W9-CFB-509

BEYOND THE BILLBOARD

BEYOND THE BILLBOARD

SUSAN GATES

Harcourt, Inc.

Orlando   Austin   New York   San Diego   Toronto   London

www.HarcourtBooks.com

First published in Great Britain by Puffin Books in 2005 as *Firebird*
First U.S. edition 2007

Library of Congress Cataloging-in-Publication Data
Gates, Susan.
Beyond the billboard/Susan Gates.
p.   cm.
Summary: Firebird and her twin brother, Ford, have always accepted their
father's isolated way of life and secluded home in the middle of a desolate
swamp until the discovery of old family secrets changes everything.
[1. Swamps—Fiction.   2. Family life—Fiction.
3. Brothers and sisters—Fiction.   4. Twins—Fiction.]   I. Title.
PZ7.G2234Bg   2007
[Fic]—dc22   2006031527
ISBN 978-0-15-205983-5

Text set in Janson
Designed by Cathy Riggs

A C E G H F D B

Printed in the United States of America

Firebird suddenly felt scared.
As if letting on that she knew the family's secrets
would be like opening Pandora's box,
bringing down death and destruction
on all their heads.

BEYOND THE BILLBOARD

1

THE eels writhed and twisted in the trap.

"Three, no four," said Ford as they winched the wire-mesh trap into the boat. "Big 'uns, Dad."

Trapper, Ford's dad, said nothing. He never talked much, not when they were eel fishing in the swamp, or at any other time for that matter. Ford didn't say too much, either. It seemed a shame to break the spell of this just-dawn time, when the light changed from gray to pretty pink. It made even the swamp look inviting. The mud sink-holes, deep enough to drown a child, seemed like innocent paddling pools.

And there was another reason Ford kept his lip buttoned. He felt proud when he was working alongside his father. He felt like a grown man even though he was just thirteen. He didn't want to spoil things with childish chatter.

He was proud, too, that his father was a legend. The best eel catcher on the swamp. Actually, the only eel catcher on the swamp now. There had once been a little community down here. But the other families had moved out, given up on this kind of life years ago. Since then, their wooden houses had fallen into ruins, been swallowed up by the swamp.

"Why'd they move on, Dad?" Ford had once asked Trapper.

According to Trapper, the eel business was booming. The smokery upriver couldn't get enough of them. And hadn't they just bought a new boat, sleek, fast, made of wood, to replace their old rubber dinghy? That proved they were making big money.

"So why did the others leave?" Ford had wanted to know. The McVeighs, the Evanses, the Seagers—they had all gone now.

Trapper had just shrugged and grinned. "Just couldn't compete with us Tuckers, I suppose."

"That's true," Ford had agreed. "We're the best."

He and Trapper made a great team. And Gran, too— she was an expert eel skinner. Firebird, his twin sister, didn't help out much though. She just wandered around the swamp. Or if she wasn't doing that, she was staring at the billboard, lost in some daydream. Ford resented it sometimes, that Firebird didn't pull her weight in the family eel-fishing business. That Dad and Gran didn't even expect her to; like somehow, she had special privileges.

Anyhow, Ford already knew his future. He was going to be an eel trapper like his dad and his granddad and his great-granddad and all the Tuckers before that. Why would he want to be anything different?

If he wasn't eaten alive by mosquitoes first. One whined by his ear, then stopped. Ford slapped at his earlobe. It was one of their favorite places for sucking blood.

Trapper dumped the eels into the plastic bucket on deck, where they thrashed about and made slime. Ford threw the grappling hook over the side, trying to locate two traps that they'd baited with crabs last night and left in the creek.

Eels hunted at night. Sometimes they even slithered out of the water and wriggled through the swamp grass. Ford had seen them do it. He'd seen one, by moonlight, nearly a yard long, take chicks from a coot's nest.

The swamp where the Tuckers lived was a little wetland wilderness. It was a maze of creeks, some like this one, wide with clear water. Others just black, silty ditches. In between the creeks were tangled islands of reeds and willow, quaking grass bogs and sundews.

Ford knew this treacherous place better than the back of his own hand. It was his personal playground, his neighborhood. He and his twin sister, Firebird, had been born here, grown up here. They'd almost never left it, not even to go to school. What did they need school for? Gran had taught them their letters and numbers.

Once a week, Trapper took the boat to buy supplies at Hook Bay, just downriver. He often took Ford with him. He'd have taken Firebird, too, if she'd wanted to go. But she almost never did.

"She's like your mom," Trapper would say approvingly, "a real home bird. Your mom loved this place. She never wanted to leave."

Trapper used to take Ford to the smokery, too, where they sold their eel catch. But he hadn't done that lately. For some reason, Trapper had taken to going to the smokery alone.

The swamp was on the edge of a wide river estuary. And somewhere that river ran into the ocean. The ocean was far away, but it still had a big effect on the swamp. Which way the current ran in the swamp creeks depended on that distant ocean, whether its tide was going out or coming in.

Trapper said eels can smell the ocean. Even though they've swum miles and miles inland, up freshwater rivers and creeks, they can still smell the salty sea where they were born. And where they'd go back to die someday, if Trapper didn't get them first.

"Bastards," said Trapper suddenly.

Ford didn't take much notice. He thought an eel had jumped out of the bucket and given his dad a nip with its razor-sharp teeth.

But Trapper cursed again. And there was so much venom in his voice that Ford hauled in the grappling hook, with no trap on the end of it, and looked around.

"What's up, Dad? Did one get you?"

But it wasn't the eels Dad was swearing at. It was a big eyeball, sticking out of the reeds.

"Recognize that?" said Trapper. "It's a webcam. They've got one in the store at Hook Bay."

He edged the boat closer, taking care not to scrape a rusty shopping cart half buried in mud. Then he cut the engine.

"Watch out, Dad," said Ford. "It'll film us."

"No, it won't," said Trapper.

The camera lens wasn't pointing at them. It seemed to be filming a big, dead tree on one of the willow islands.

"So they came back, did they?" said Trapper, suddenly talkative. "Sneaking in here, setting up cameras, in *my* swamp. Wish I'd caught them," he told Ford in a voice thick with fury. "I'd have taught them a lesson they'd *never* forget."

2

WHEN Trapper and Ford found the webcam, Firebird was sitting where she often sat, staring at the billboard.

There was a roaring sound in her ears. That sound never went away; the Tuckers heard it day and night. Like the rest of her family, Firebird was hardly aware of it. But sometimes, when it kept her from getting to sleep, she liked to imagine it was the sound of the distant ocean, of its great foamy breakers crashing onto the shore.

Suddenly, an earsplitting scream came from the sky. A Boeing 747 shot by low overhead, heading for the airport. It made the swamp water ripple and the grasses shiver even after it had gone.

Firebird didn't look up. It happened a hundred times a day. And that ever-present roar in her ears wasn't the ocean, as Firebird liked to pretend. It was an eight-lane highway, a concrete tangle of over- and underpasses where traffic thundered by twenty-four hours a day—if it wasn't gridlocked, that is.

The subway trains were noisy, too. But they made a different rattling sound as they rushed over the iron bridges. Beyond the roads and train tracks, the city started. Often a haze of pollution hid it. But when the smog lifted, it sprawled as far as the eye could see.

The swamp was on the extreme edge of the city, its last wild margin. Almost crushed out of existence as the city closed in. But somehow, it was still clinging on.

Trapper hated the city with a fierce, unforgiving hatred. He wanted nothing to do with it. He tried to act as if it didn't exist. As if it were some kind of mirage or virtual-reality illusion, even though his ears were filled with its constant clamor.

Gran didn't seem to mind the city as much as Trapper. She always said, "We're the pimple on the city's backside." But sometimes she'd add, "Yeah, and one day they're going to scratch us."

But it hadn't happened so far. No one from the city had bothered the Tuckers. There was no vehicle access, no trails to walk to the swamp. It was almost impossible to reach, except by boat. And if any city dweller did come snooping down here, through the stinking subways, the derelict buildings, across the eight-lane highway, over the rail tracks, big DANGER signs warned them not to go any farther.

But it was the billboard that protected the Tuckers the most. It plugged the gap between scrubby hills and screened the swamp from prying eyes. It sheltered their home behind it like the wall of a medieval fortress. The billboard was gigantic, towering, as long as the longest highway freight truck, twice as high as their house.

It needed to be massive so the people in cars wouldn't miss it as they sped by. And that's as far as their glances went. Their eyes always stopped at the ad. They probably never, ever wondered what was behind it. Even the men who came every month and pasted up new posters, with long ladders and brushes, weren't curious. They just did their job and went back to the city.

The billboard made Firebird and her family invisible. They were as hidden behind it as some lost tribe deep in the Amazon jungle—with a way of life that would seem, to city dwellers, just as strange and primitive. And it hid the city from them, too. Except for the tops of its tallest sky-scrapers. Even the billboard couldn't shut out those soaring glass towers, some a third of a mile high. At night they were lit up. Firebird could see them from her bedroom window. They glowed ghostly blue or fiery red. One—the tallest—had a roving beam on top. Every night it circled the city like a giant searchlight. Its dazzling brightness out-shone the moon and the stars.

"LIVE YOUR DREAMS!" said Firebird out loud. She was sitting cross-legged in the long grass, gazing up at the billboard and reading its message.

It seemed like a personal message from the billboard to her, meant for her eyes alone, even though a million com-muters saw it every day.

Firebird was wiry, skinny, tanned, with a lion's mane of wild, gingery hair. She looked much younger than thirteen years old. The billboard was the limit of her world. Every day, from the swamp, she saw its gray back, crisscrossed with wooden struts, shielding her family: A barrier between them and the city.

Most days Firebird crawled underneath the billboard to get to the city side, so she could sit and study the ads.

Firebird had read her first words from those ads. The billboard had been like her own giant-sized picture book, with bright, shouting colors and huge letters taller than she was. Other kids read words like *cat* or *dog* in their baby books. The first words Firebird learned were Nike, Coke, Microsoft, and Campbell's Creamy Tomato Soup.

She was even named after an ad, as Gran had told her a million times. The ad that had been on the billboard the day she was born.

"It was a flashy red car," said Gran, "called a Firebird. And what with you having red hair. And your mom being named from the billboard, too . . ."

"Who said that should be my name?" Firebird often asked. It didn't matter that she already knew; she just liked hearing the story. And Gran was a wonderful storyteller.

"I did," said Gran, "what with your poor mother dying like that soon after you and Ford were born. And your dad being so brokenhearted. Someone had to name you."

So, one way or another, the billboard played a big part in Firebird's life. She couldn't imagine it ever not being there.

The poster that was up there right now fascinated her. When the men came to tear it down and paste up a fresh one, she knew she would really miss it.

"LIVE YOUR DREAMS!" the poster on the billboard

commanded her, in black letters so tall that when she gazed up at them she felt dizzy.

It was an ad for a travel company. Around its urgent message were pictures of faraway places. Of beaches and forests and snowcapped mountains and jeweled palaces with onion-shaped domes. Places much better than the swamp, or boring old Hook Bay.

Firebird imagined herself walking those beaches, climbing those mountains, wandering, wide-eyed, around those palaces. But she knew she was just kidding herself.

She looked toward the city hidden in smog like a mystical, cloud-draped island. It was four, maybe five miles away. But she'd never even been there. She was as far beyond the billboard, just a few feet, as she was ever likely to get.

Suddenly, Firebird leaped up from the grass and shook herself like a dog. She wriggled back under the billboard and ran along one of the twisty paths that cut through the head-high reeds.

I don't want to go there, anyway! she told herself fiercely.

Did she mean to the city? Or to one of those places she'd seen on the billboard? It couldn't be the city she wanted to go to. Trapper had warned her off it, ever since she could remember. He'd say, over and over again, "We've got all we need here. The city's a terrible place."

And Firebird would say, because she knew it was what Trapper wanted to hear, "I don't ever want to go there, Dad. I'm going to stay here, with you and Gran."

Then Trapper's face would light up with pleasure and he'd say, "Just like your mom."

But sometimes, like today, Firebird got restless. She felt twitchy, like she had an itch she couldn't scratch. She longed for *something*, but she hardly knew what it was.

"What's *wrong* with you?" Firebird asked herself, exasperated.

She had to go and see Mom's angel. That would calm her down, get things sorted out in her mind.

3

FORD watched Trapper anxiously. Ford worshipped his dad, wanted to be just like him. But it wasn't the strong, silent, capable Trapper he was seeing now. This seemed like another person.

Trapper's face was twisted with fury. He was spitting out words, but so fast, so choked with anger, that Ford could hardly understand.

"Interfering—!" raved Trapper. "Coming down here to *my* swamp, telling me I got no right to fish here!"

Trapper flung his arm out so wildly that he almost slipped on the slime and blood and eel guts that slicked the deck boards. For once he was acknowledging the city, stabbing his finger at the tops of its distant towers crowding the sky.

"Why don't they stay back there where they belong?"

"Who, Dad, who?" begged Ford frantically. "Who're you *talking* about? Is it whoever set up this webcam?"

But Trapper was in no mood for explanations. He'd just picked up the grappling hook. And Ford knew, from the look on Dad's face, that he wasn't about to hook eel traps with it. Trapper was taking deep breaths, as if he was psyching himself up for something. His whole body was shaking violently, with a mixture of fury and excitement and nervous tension.

"What are you gonna do, Dad?"

"See that webcam?" demanded Trapper. "See the solar panel that powers it? You just watch what I'm going to do, boy. You just watch me!"

The solar panel glittered like blue glass in the sunshine. The eyeball lens of the webcam looked away, focused on the dead tree.

Trapper swung the grappling hook. The boat swayed as he swiped at the solar panel. It cracked like a car windshield.

It was already beyond repair. But Trapper wasn't finished. In a frenzy, he hit it again and again, shattering the cells into blue fragments. He seemed to want it in a million pieces.

Ford clung on as the boat rocked and creek water sloshed over the sides.

"Dad, Dad, you'll sink us!"

But Trapper couldn't hear. Panting heavily now, he swung the grappling hook again, mouthing curses. He'd lost all reason. If he were a dog, he'd be foaming at the mouth.

"Dad!" Ford slid along the bottom of the boat, grabbed Trapper's legs. "Dad, stop, it's all smashed up."

Trapper looked down as if he was surprised to see his son clinging to his ankles. He stopped in mid swipe and shook his head savagely as if to clear it. He stared at the hook in his hands, then at the wrecked solar panel. He shook his head again.

And then, suddenly, he was back to the dad Ford knew. Carefully, as if it were made of fragile glass, he laid the grappling hook down. He looked directly at Ford. His voice was calm and level again.

"That'll teach 'em," he said. "Teach 'em they can't mess with us Tuckers."

He hauled up the anchor, started the outboard, and pulled away. In seconds they were hidden in one of the reedy channels. Trapper sat down on the upturned crates they used as seats. Ford noticed that his father's hands were shaking.

But then Trapper lit a cigarette, took a few heavy drags, and the trembling in his hands stopped.

Ford stared at him. His dad was behaving just like normal, as if the attack on the solar panel had never happened. *Did I really see that?* Ford thought. His shy, uncommunicative dad going berserk, out of control?

But Trapper wasn't saying anything. He was his usual quiet, steady-as-a-rock self, just like all the other times when they went out eel trapping. But this time Ford had to break the silence between them.

"Who put the webcam there, Dad? Do you know?"

Trapper cut the engine, let the boat drift. He looked at the eels, writhing around in the bucket making slime. He looked down at the still-burning cigarette dangling from his fingers and sighed. It was a sigh so lonesome, so deep and hopeless, that Ford's heart reached out to him. He wanted to say something comforting. But he couldn't find the right words. Instead his heart just hammered with anxiety and confusion and he ended up begging, "Dad, what's going on?"

At last, Trapper lifted his head. Ford was relieved to see that his gray eyes were angry again. Not that Ford *liked* to see Trapper get angry. And he'd *never* seen him in a fit of crazy, destructive rage like just now. But somehow he preferred even that, a thousand times over, to despair.

"We've got trouble," said Trapper. "They're trying to take over the swamp, drive us out."

"Who is?" asked Ford.

Trapper took another long pull on his cigarette. He seemed to be thinking, turning over in his mind how much to tell his son. Ford saw that he was stroking the old scar on his cheek. He always did that when he was worried.

Trapper was a very private man, paranoid about it. He hated people poking their noses into the Tuckers' lives. Most of all, he hated people from the city.

"I met these two guys," he said, "last week."

"Where was I?" asked Ford. He was almost always with his father, except when Trapper went to the smokery.

Dad shrugged, as if that wasn't important. "You were doing something for Gran," he said. "Anyway, I was out checking traps and these two guys came sneaking up on me in a rubber dinghy. At first, I thought they were duck hunting. But they didn't have guns. Then one said, 'What are you doing here? You'll disturb the fish eagle.'"

"What fish eagle?" asked Ford. He and Dad knew all the wildlife in the swamp; every heron, bittern, and water rat.

"Well, that's just what I said. I told 'em, 'There isn't a fish eagle. You don't see those this far north.' So these two guys look at me like I was something they'd trod on and the one with the beard says, 'We heard there is. That it's nesting in that tree over there.' And the other guy butts in and says, 'There are lots of new species coming up here that you wouldn't expect. You never heard about global warming?' So I just laughed at that and said, 'Don't believe in it.' So then Beardface, he gets nasty. He says, 'You got permission to fish here?'"

Ford looked bewildered. Why would they need permission to fish in their own swamp? Tuckers had been fishing here, Gran said, for three hundred years. They'd been here first, before the city was even thought of, when there were just a few eel fishers' shacks.

"Did you tell these two guys to get lost, Dad? Get out of our swamp?"

Trapper wouldn't think twice about telling intruders to get lost. Only he didn't say get lost—he wasn't so polite.

Ford was disappointed when Dad grimaced and said, "No. I did some groveling—I wanted to find out why they were nosing around. I said, 'I don't need permission, do I?' And they said, 'You soon will, when we get control of this site. You'll need a license even to *be* here.'"

"Come on, Dad! Were they joking or something?"

Ford almost started to laugh. But he saw Trapper was dead

serious and the laughter died in his throat. "They can't do that," said Ford. But now there was a tremor of doubt in his voice.

"They can," said Trapper, stubbing out his cigarette on the deck boards, grinding it in with his heel. "Turns out they're from the FWS, the Fish and Wildlife Service. And they've got their eye on this place. They want to turn it into a wildlife reserve. *Manage* it," said Trapper with a bitter laugh. "That's what they said they're going to do. *Manage* it."

"But why's that so bad?" asked Ford, not understanding.

"Because the first thing they'll manage is *us*," said Trapper. "They'll kick us out, in case we 'disturb the wildlife.'"

Ford thought about this. Then he burst out desperately, "You sure, Dad? Maybe they'll let us stay. Didn't you ask them?"

Trapper shook his head. "I don't want them to know we live here. What if the tax people come snooping, or the truancy officers?"

So far the Tuckers hadn't come to the notice of any officials. As far as the city was concerned, the family didn't exist. Trapper wanted it to stay that way.

"But it's just talk, isn't it, Dad, about them taking over the swamp?" Ford knew there'd been scares like that before. "What about that time they wanted to build the new airport here?" Ford reminded Trapper. "That never happened, did it?"

But Trapper didn't give Ford the reassurance he so desperately needed. Instead, he said, "Anyhow, I think that's what that webcam is all about. They're trying to prove there's some valuable wildlife down here. Rare stuff that needs protecting."

"Then we don't need to worry!" said Ford, feeling relief fizzing inside him. "Because there isn't any rare stuff, is there, Dad? Just some scabby old rats and seagulls, and who cares about those?"

"Well, there isn't any fish eagle, that's for sure," said Trapper. "All that crap about new species migrating here because of global warming—that's just because they want to get control of this place."

"So everything's all right then, isn't it, Dad?" said Ford, willing Trapper to say yes. Just the thought of being made to leave the security of the swamp horrified Ford. Where would he go? What would he do? How would he survive in the world? His future, even his identity, seemed threatened.

For a second, Ford was close to panic. All the cool he tried to maintain when he was working alongside Trapper, doing a grown man's job, almost got snatched away. In his heart, he felt like a frightened child.

Trapper was back to his old, taciturn self now, scrubbing at that scar on his cheek again. It went from just under his eye to his jaw. It had happened years ago when the winch wire on the boat snapped and slashed across his face like a whip.

"Maybe I shouldn't have smashed that solar panel," muttered Trapper, frowning. He wasn't even looking at

Ford; he seemed to be speaking to himself. "I just lost it. Got carried away. Maybe I shouldn't have."

"No!" insisted Ford. "You did the right thing, Dad. It's our swamp. They should leave us alone."

"We don't *own* this place, son, you know that," said Trapper. "The way they see it, we're no better than squatters."

Trapper seemed weary, his shoulders slumped. For a minute it seemed like he'd lost all his fighting spirit. His head was down; he was scratching at a mosquito bite on his ankle. Frantically, Ford pulled at Trapper's arm, made him look up.

He searched his dad's face for some reassurance. Trapper had a sudden violent shivering fit, as if someone were walking over his grave. Then he seemed to recover. He lit another cigarette.

"Don't worry," he told Ford. "Nobody's going to drive us out. If they try, we'll stop 'em, whoever they are."

"Yeah, Dad!" Ford felt ecstatic, excited. He leaped up, punched the air, making the boat rock. "Me and you, we'll fight 'em. I'm not scared of them. I'm not scared of nobody."

Trapper grinned. "Well, you ought to be. You know what your gran's like. She'll skin us quicker than an eel if we're late for breakfast."

Early morning fog still hung about in patches. Trapper steered them back through the reedy channels. Little fish flashed and glittered under the boat. A heron flapped up from some hidden, misty pool.

In the background, the traffic noise never let up. Horns

blared, trains rattled, ambulance and police sirens wailed. But Ford didn't even hear them. Like Trapper, he could blank out the city. He didn't care about anything beyond the billboard. He wasn't like Firebird—he never went around the other side to look at the ads.

All he cared about was right here.

4

FIREBIRD ran along Whiskey Creek and made a left turn by the smaller, siltier Willow Creek. Most of the creeks in the swamp had names. They weren't names you'd find on any map. They were known only to the people who lived here, passed down through generations of eel trappers.

The reason for some of the names had been long forgotten. There was Judith's Creek. Now no one, not even Gran, knew who Judith was or why she had a creek named after her. But Flood Creek, that was easy to explain. In stormy weather, when the river rose, that was the creek it came surging in by, in a wall of tumbling brown foam. Then you had to run for your life, take refuge in the house, and hope that didn't get washed away, too.

And Witch Creek—Gran had told Firebird the reason for that name. Sometimes balls of spooky blue fire danced over Witch Creek. Firebird had seen them herself. Trapper said it was marsh gas, but Gran said they were witch lights. That a witch was lurking in the reeds, rolling those blue balls out to tempt the swamp children, hoping a child would think *What a pretty thing!* and run to catch one.

"And then," Gran would say, "that witch pounced. She'd got 'em!"

The witch dragged the child off to her den in the thickest reeds. "So if you see a pretty blue ball, Firebird," Gran would say, "just think of that old witch and never, ever run toward it. Run like hell the other way."

Firebird had believed that when she was small. For a long time she'd fled in terror from witch lights.

Gran had loads of stories about the swamp. And she had no qualms about scaring her grandchildren stupid. Gran knew all about the Tucker family, too. She was like a talking history book. Only, unlike a history book, Gran never had much use for dates. Months, even years, don't mean much in a swamp, where every day is the same. When things *did* happen, Gran marked them by what had been up on the billboard.

"When you and Ford cut your first teeth," she'd say, "that was when the Inland Revenue ad was up there. And it was Wash 'n' Go shampoo when your dad had that accident with the winch wire."

By now, Firebird had almost reached Mom's angel. The narrow track between the reeds was boggy, oozing water like a sponge. Firebird leaped over a vivid patch of green. It looked mossy and inviting. It seemed to be saying, "Step on me!" But Firebird knew that if you tried, you would plunge straight through the floating weed into the black water beneath. The swamp was full of traps for the unwary. Even Firebird had to be careful. No Tucker ever took their safety for granted. You had to respect the swamp, never forget that it could kill you.

A helicopter buzzed overhead. It wasn't interested in the swamp. It was probably heading for the city to report on traffic snarl-ups for a local radio station. It swooped away to hover over the skyscrapers.

Firebird pushed her way through a patch of sunflowers. Their bright yellow heads, big as dinner plates, drooped above her. It was strange, those sunflowers—they'd never grown in the swamp before. Then one day, there they were, springing up like weeds!

"Didn't think they grew this far north," Gran had said.

A butterfly settled on a sunflower. Firebird stopped to stare at it. It was a gorgeous, exotic creature, striped orange and black, with swallowtail wings. *Where'd that come from?* thought Firebird. Like the sunflowers, it was a new arrival, unlike anything she'd seen before. She made a mental note to tell Gran about it when she got back home.

Firebird stopped by a little inlet overhung with willows. Mom's angel lay on her back in the creek among the clamshells. You couldn't see all of her wings; they were buried in mud. You could just see some stone feathers, sprouting from her shoulder blades.

Firebird pushed her tangled hair out of her eyes and scrubbed at her grimy face to smarten herself up a bit. Then she kneeled to look down through the clear water. The angel stared back, with wide-open eyes.

The angel was a life-sized stone statue. Dad had put her there after Mom died. She was Mom's memorial, hidden in the creek, in the heart of the swamp, so snooping strangers wouldn't find her.

One of the fingers of her praying hands was missing. Somehow, her dress had got damaged, too; it was chipped and cracked in a dozen places. But it didn't matter. When you saw her through the water, with all the distorting ripples and refractions, she looked perfect.

"Trapper sunk her in the creek," went Gran's story. "And you know what he said as he did it? He said, 'An angel for an angel.' Because your mom was an angel when she was here on earth. And now she's an angel up in heaven."

Gran said Trapper had had the angel specially made. It must have cost a fortune. Firebird once asked Gran how Dad got the angel here, how she didn't sink his boat. And if he damaged her on the way—because she was a bit knocked about. But Gran shook her head irritably, as if silly details like that didn't matter. So Firebird never asked again. She was just proud that Mom had such a fine memorial.

"He sunk it at Loreal's favorite spot," said Gran.

Loreal, that was Mom's name, from a hair spray ad on the billboard. "Lovely name, isn't it?" Gran would always say.

Loreal was an Evans, who had stayed behind in the swamp when the rest of her family moved out, because she couldn't bear to leave. She was so much in love with the swamp and with Trapper.

Visiting Mom's angel was a stern reminder to Firebird of where her duty lay. She struggled to crush that restlessness inside her. It was a betrayal of Mom even feeling that way. Loreal would have been happy, Gran said, to spend her whole life here in the swamp if she hadn't died tragically in childbirth. Loreal had never wanted anything else.

Firebird stood in respectful silence looking down at Mom's angel. At the drapes of her long, stone gown, her bare toes—two missing—poking out from beneath them. She had a wreath of stone roses around her head. Her wide-open eyes were blank, white disks, empty of all expression.

There were no photos of Loreal. And whenever Firebird tried to imagine what her dead mother had looked like, she always mixed her up with the angel. So, in Firebird's mind, Mom had the same blank, beautiful face.

Firebird had been terrified of that statue when she was little, staring up at her from the creek like a drowned person. Until she'd been taught it was Mom's special memorial and how she mustn't be scared.

"Why can't you be happy?" Firebird asked herself angrily, remembering how restless she'd felt at the billboard that morning.

She sat down on a chunk of gray stone, carved with leaves, at the edge of the creek. It made a handy, sun-warmed seat.

Gran and Trapper were always saying how Firebird took after Mom, how Mom would have been proud of her. But Firebird knew that wasn't true. If she'd been like Mom, she wouldn't feel so discontented most of the time. She was a bad daughter. And you just couldn't be a bad daughter to a mom who'd died giving birth to you and whose memory Dad worshipped. And who was an angel in heaven.

"This swamp was her whole world; she never wanted to

leave," Trapper would say. And then he'd always add, "She wouldn't have wanted you to, either."

Sometimes Firebird secretly thought that living up to an angel was a terrible burden. She got sick of hearing Gran and Trapper talk about Loreal as if she was just *so* perfect. And resentful that a mom she'd never known was dictating her future even from beyond the grave: "You will stay in the swamp forever. You *will* be happy here!" But then Firebird felt bad for thinking that way. And resolved, yet again, to try to be a good daughter.

Today, even paying a visit to Mom's angel didn't give Firebird's troubled mind any peace. The billboard's message still echoed in her head: "LIVE YOUR DREAMS!" Trouble was, Firebird wasn't even sure yet what her dreams were.

A cold, wet nose pressed into her hand.

"Swamp Dog," said Firebird, patting his wet, seal-like head.

Swamp Dog was half-feral, too wild and too scared of humans even to have a proper dog's name. He was a stray from beyond the billboard. But he was a swamp dog now. He didn't scavenge in city streets anymore or rip open garbage bags. He swam across creeks like a water snake, scarcely making a ripple. He crunched crabs, raided moorhens' nests, and fought with the squawking seagulls for the fish guts Trapper threw from the boat.

The only human he'd ever approach was Firebird.

"Where've you been?" said Firebird, picking slimy strands of weed off his head. "I haven't seen you since the Bacardi Breezer ad."

Swamp Dog cringed, as if he expected to be hit. He always did that, trembled and crawled on his belly, even with Firebird, who would never hurt him. You never made any sudden moves with Swamp Dog. If you did, or if something else scared him, he was off like a rocket.

He did that now. He took off like a hare. Firebird saw his skinny haunches wriggling into the reeds. Then he was gone.

Firebird looked around for what had scared him. A jumbo jet had just screamed overhead. But, like the rest of the city noise that surrounded them, Swamp Dog must have gotten used to that by now.

Suddenly, Firebird froze. The bow of an unfamiliar boat was nosing its way down the creek. Why hadn't the chug of an engine warned her? Then Firebird saw that the boat was a canoe being paddled.

"Hey!" called a woman's voice, a stranger.

Firebird sprang up from the bank. She'd been about to flee into the reeds, but it was too late: She'd been spotted. Instinctively, she moved away from Loreal's angel, who lay in dappled shadow under the willows.

The woman in the canoe had a bright orange life jacket on over trousers and a long-sleeved T-shirt. Underneath her wide, floppy sun hat, there was a concerned look on her face.

"What are you doing here?" she said to Firebird. "This swamp is a dangerous place for children. Didn't you see the signs?"

Firebird didn't answer, just watched the woman warily. She'd been warned about strangers by Dad a million times.

They didn't often find their way into the swamp. But if they did, you didn't let them see you; you hid in the reeds until they'd gone. Firebird had broken that rule already. And if they spoke to you, asked you questions, you never answered. You just acted dumb.

"Then run home, soon as you can," Dad always said.

But Firebird was breaking that rule, too. She could have run, wriggled into the reeds like Swamp Dog, where the woman could never have followed. But she didn't.

Now the woman was smiling at her, curious but friendly. Firebird almost let her defenses down and smiled back.

But instead, she acted dumb, like Dad had told her. She stared at the woman as if she didn't understand her questions.

"You on your own down here?" asked the woman.

Firebird said nothing. Just swatted away a mosquito that was whining by her ear.

The woman said, "Is it my imagination? Or are these mosquitoes bigger and biting fiercer this summer? Glad I covered up, put on plenty of repellent."

Firebird didn't let a flicker of understanding cross her face. The woman frowned and shrugged. "Well, okay, if you don't want to talk." She swatted at the mosquitoes, too, and started to paddle away from the angel toward another creek.

Firebird's heart stopped fluttering. She watched the canoe skimming over the water. She breathed easily again. She prepared to do what she should have done in the first place—escape into the reeds.

But then the woman, gazing back at Firebird one last time, saw something else.

Her eyes widened. "It can't be," she said, paddling back.

Shit, thought Firebird, who'd learned to curse from Trapper. *She isn't leaving.*

Firebird's heart cramped in her chest. What had the stranger seen? Was it the angel?

Firebird checked back upstream. The angel was well submerged. But what if the woman paddled a little and pushed aside the willow curtain? Looked down through the water and saw that stone face staring up?

But it wasn't the angel. Something else had grabbed the woman's attention. She'd stopped her canoe by the lump of stone Firebird had been sitting on. She seemed really excited, reaching out, tracing the leafy pattern with her fingers, as if it were a precious object.

"Wow!" she said. "I can't believe it!"

Firebird tried to keep up her dumb act. But her eyes darted nervously from the woman to the chunk of stone and back again. She wanted desperately to escape, but she didn't dare. She didn't want this stranger finding the angel. That was Mom's memorial, a private, sacred place, just for family, not for a stranger's prying eyes.

The woman's gaze was roving farther up the creek. "There any more bits of stone like this?" she asked Firebird. "With carvings or letters on them?"

Reluctantly, Firebird spoke. She said no, hoping it would make the woman go away.

If Trapper came along, he'd soon get rid of her. He wouldn't waste time listening to stupid questions. He'd say, "Look, just get lost, lady. Can't you see I'm busy?" Trapper was suspicious of all strangers in his swamp. "Don't trust any of them," he'd warn Firebird. "They'll tell you a pack of lies."

But the woman didn't go away. Instead, she took out a little digital camera and started taking pictures of the lump of stone.

Why's she doing that? thought Firebird. The woman seemed really excited about the stone, like it had made her day. Like someone had given her a big birthday present.

"I'm almost certain that's part of a gravestone," said the woman. "Maybe even part of a tomb. I'll have to double-check, of course, back at the department."

"What department?" asked Firebird, frowning.

Trapper hated departments. Departments meant officials. Officials who thought they had a God-given right to poke their noses into your private business.

The woman's gaze swung back to her, as if she'd forgotten Firebird was there.

"The Archaeology Department, at the university. I'm Dr. Pinker, by the way, Dr. Linda Pinker. And I'm almost certain this piece of stone is an important part of our city's architectural heritage. It's from an old church that used to be right where the city center is now."

Firebird, with a sudden flash of anger, said, "You better ask my dad if you can take those photos."

"Your dad?" said Dr. Pinker. "What's he got to do with it? Does he have any authority down here?"

Firebird clamped her mouth shut. She'd already said too much. What had Trapper told her? If strangers get nosy, act dumb. Never give anything away. Firebird stared down stubbornly at her shoes.

Dr. Pinker shrugged. She took another snap and shook her head as if she still couldn't believe her luck.

Above her, another exotic, tiger-striped butterfly drifted by. But Dr. Pinker was too excited about the stone to notice.

"Architectural vandalism," frowned Dr. Pinker, shaking her head. "Wouldn't be allowed now. But this was a long time ago. Anyhow, when they pulled down the church, cleared the graveyard to put up new buildings, they dumped the rubble right here in the swamp. It's so exciting! I only found the evidence yesterday, from old records and photos. There was a photo of an angel . . ."

She stopped. Firebird was finally raising her head. Dr. Pinker mistook the gleam in her eyes for interest.

She asked eagerly, "You seen a stone angel around here? Because I'd really like to find her. She came from somebody's grave. In the old photos, it looks like she's got a wreath of roses round her head. Course it's a real long shot. She probably got damaged in the demolition. And if she was in this swamp, she'd have been here a hundred years, at least . . ."

From behind her long, tangled hair, Firebird shot the woman a glare of pure hatred.

"If the angel *is* here," continued Dr. Pinker, "it's important to find her. What with global warming and rising water levels, this swamp'll be part of the river in no time. We need to take her away as soon as we can."

"Take her away?" repeated Firebird, her voice stunned, disbelieving. "Where to?"

"My department," said Dr. Pinker. "We could put her on display there, so lots of people could see her."

Suddenly, Firebird transformed. One second she was a shy, sullen kid. The next she was a screeching fury. She bunched her hands into fists, shrieking wildly, "You go away. You get lost. We don't want you here!"

Then she flung herself at the canoe, trying to push it away from the bank.

Shocked, and even a little scared, Dr. Pinker said, "Hey! Calm down!" She grasped her paddle for a quick getaway. "I only asked you about an angel."

Now Firebird, her face twisted with rage and distress, was rocking the canoe.

Dr. Pinker yelled, "Let go! Are you crazy?"

Firebird let go for a second, squatted back on her heels on the bank to scream again, "Go away! Go away!"

Dr. Pinker saw her chance to escape. She steadied the canoe, spun it, began to paddle as fast as she could back down the creek.

Firebird chased Dr. Pinker down the bank like a guard dog seeing off an intruder. "There aren't no stone angels round here!"

Finally, Firebird skidded to a stop. The orange life jacket had vanished in the reeds. Dr. Pinker was leaving the swamp.

Firebird sat down on the bank, panting and shaking. For the first time the implications of what Dr. Pinker said really hit her. She scowled and shook her head, puzzled.

How could the angel have come from some city graveyard, when Dad had it specially made for Mom? How could it have been in the swamp for a hundred years, when Dad brought it here thirteen years ago?

Firebird didn't pursue these questions. They were too disturbing. *That's crap, what that Dr. Pinker was saying*, she told herself. *About stuff being dumped here from some city church.*

All the same, Firebird found herself hiding the lump of stone with the carved leaves under some ripped-off willow branches, so that if any more archaeologists came snooping, they wouldn't find it.

5

GRAN was skinning the eels Ford and Trapper had caught that morning, whacking them on the landing stage to kill them, then pinning them by their heads to the wooden wall of the house. One quick slash around the necks with her skinning knife to free the skin, then she stripped it off whole, neat as a stocking.

There were lots of eel skins pegged to a washing line to dry in the sun. Once they'd lost that slime and wetness, they looked totally different, even beautiful, like fragile, transparent flags shimmering in rainbow colors. But they were much tougher than they looked. You could even stitch them together, make them into things. What was left of the eels, once they'd been skinned and gutted, would be taken to the smokery by Trapper.

"They're fetching a high price now," Trapper had told Ford after his last trip, folding a big wad of money away in his wallet. "Eel fishing is the business to be in."

And Ford had nodded wisely. "Sure is."

The Tuckers' house, hidden behind the billboard, was raised on stilts in case the creek flooded. It was roofed with reeds, so from the air it couldn't be spotted, either. It had no electricity supply. Trapper was scared the thumping of a generator might lead to their discovery. So the Tuckers used oil lamps at night and wood to fuel their stove.

The yard outside was a dump because eel trapping is a messy and bloody business. It was a jumble of old wire eel traps, ropes, plastic barrels, and fuel cans. Drying eel skins fluttered in the wind. There was a crusher on the landing stage where Gran smashed up the horseshoe crabs that they used as bait.

But inside, the house was a little palace, spotlessly scrubbed and tidy. Gran was a ferocious housekeeper. The worst crime was to come into the house with your rubber boots on, all filthy with eel slime and fish scales, and mess up Gran's nice clean floors.

As Gran deftly skinned eels, Ford told her about the FWS guys who'd set up the webcam for some fish eagle that was supposed to have moved to the swamp because of global warming. "You ever heard anything so stupid?" said Ford.

Gran didn't reply.

"Yeah, and Dad smashed their solar panel to pieces," Ford went on, his eyes gleaming approval. "Those guys won't be back in a hurry."

This time Gran did react. She threw a raised eyebrow glance at Trapper, who shrugged as if it was no big deal. But then rubbed at the scar on his cheek.

"Did you have to do that?" said Gran, as if she was talking to a little kid and not her thirty-year-old son. "Did you have to be so damn hotheaded?"

"*Aww*, don't tell him off, Gran," begged Ford, leaping to Dad's defense like he always did. "Who do they think they are, coming into our swamp, setting up webcams like they own the place?"

But Gran gave a flick of her head. "Go inside," she ordered Ford. "Take some eel skins to your sister."

Ford protested. "No way! She can get them for herself."

He didn't like Gran bossing him about, treating him like a child, when he did a grown man's job, bringing money into the house.

But you didn't mess with Gran. Gran was fifty-two years old, a big woman, strong and energetic. She'd been widowed long ago, in her twenties, when Trapper's dad was drowned coming back from Hook Bay. His boat capsized in a sudden, freak storm. The boat got washed up, but his body was never found.

Gran had a loud voice for yelling above the highway traffic, hard hands, and sharp eyes that didn't miss a trick. Ford wanted to stand up to her but he knew he'd get a crack around the ear if he stepped too far out of line. He appealed to Trapper. "Dad, why can't Firebird get her own stuff? It's just for those stupid purses she makes," he added scornfully.

But, to his dismay, Trapper didn't back him up. "Just do what your gran says," growled Trapper, not even making eye contact.

Ford didn't get the eel skins off the line. They were too

dry and brittle. They had to be greased, made soft and supple by Gran, before Firebird could use them. Instead, he picked a pile of prepared skins off the top of an old fuel drum.

He stomped resentfully toward the house. It bothered him that Gran went to all this trouble just so Firebird could waste time on her useless purses. Gran treated each one like it was precious, wrapped it in tissue paper, and locked it away in an old cupboard in her bedroom.

That cupboard must be nearly bursting with purses by now, thought Ford. His twin sister was always making them, if she wasn't wandering around the swamp or staring at the billboard with that dreamy, otherworldly look on her face.

Yeah, thought Ford bitterly. *She just does what she feels like while we're slaving our guts out.* Firebird should grow up, like he'd had to, make herself useful around the place.

And the thing that rankled Ford most was that Gran and Dad didn't seem to mind it. They even encouraged it—Ford couldn't understand that. Gran and Dad were real hard workers. They expected him to be; he never got thanked. How could they stand seeing Firebird, messing about like a little kid, making stupid purses out of eel skins and feathers? And every time she finished one, Gran would make a big fuss. "That's beautiful, Firebird. That's your best yet." And lock it away in her cupboard, with all the rest.

You'd think Gran would say, at least sometimes, "Get off your backside, Firebird. Skin some eels, crush some crabs, help me around the house. Do something *useful* for a change."

Ford clumped up the flight of steps to the back door. "Boots!" came Gran's warning voice.

Ford gave a deep, grumbling sigh, climbed out of his rubber boots, and went into the kitchen in his socks.

Behind him, he could hear Dad and Gran talking to each other in low, urgent voices. They seemed to be arguing about something.

The yard this time of day was in the full glare of the sun, but the house was a cool, dim refuge. If you ignored the constant traffic rumble, it seemed like the city wasn't there at all.

The net screens over the open windows kept the big, buzzing flies out and most of the mosquitoes. Ford padded in his socks over to the table where Firebird was sitting, her head bent over her work, the light filtering through the screens making her hair and face glow.

"Here!" he growled, dumping the eel skins on the table.

The feathers Firebird used to decorate her purses whirled up from the table and drifted back down again in an airy dance of red, yellow, and metallic blue.

"I'm running out of feathers," said Firebird, without looking up.

"So? What do you expect me to do about it?" said Ford. "I'm not your servant. Ask Gran to get you some."

He went padding back through the kitchen. He wanted to get outside again, hear what Gran and Trapper were talking about. Trapper seemed really jumpy lately, like he was expecting something bad to happen.

It can't be those FWS guys, thought Ford. After what

Trapper did to their solar panel, they wouldn't dare show their faces around here again.

"They'd better not," muttered Ford, clenching his fists.

When he got back outside, he was relieved to see that Gran and Trapper weren't at each other's throats. But there was a tense silence as if what they'd been arguing about wasn't settled yet. Gran was packing the skinned and gutted eels into boxes and handing them to Trapper, down in the boat.

"Want any crushed ice in those boxes, Gran?" asked Ford. "Want me to fetch some for you?"

Gran shook her head. "No, there's no need."

"But . . . ," began Ford. Before, when he went to the smokery with Dad, they'd always packed the eels in ice to keep them fresh. He couldn't understand why it would be different now.

"I told you," said Gran, anticipating his question, "we don't need ice. It's not far to the smokery."

Ford kept his mouth shut. He knew better than to cross Gran. And maybe she was right. Why waste good ice if you didn't need to?

"See you later," said Dad, starting the outboard, heading out into the creek.

Ford gazed after him. He'd stopped asking whether he could go with Trapper, like he used to. Trapper always said no. And when Ford asked him why not, Trapper answered, "I want someone to stay here, look after Gran and Firebird." That made Ford feel proud and worried at the same time. Proud because his father was treating him like a man, giving him responsibility, but worried because how could he tell Gran what to do? She was head of the whole family, even above Trapper.

Dad's boat turned a bend in the creek and disappeared, heading for the open river.

Ford sighed, turned away from the swamp, and looked west. Beyond the billboard, you could see a cluster of glittering glass towers. The helicopter still hung like a yellow teardrop over them, checking out the traffic in the city streets.

You couldn't see any actual people. Sometimes it seemed to Ford that if he ever went to the city, there would be no people there at all. That the buildings would be empty shells, the pavements deserted, the cars driverless. That the city just ran on its own, like some weird living organism.

The city was so powerful, it could even make its own weather. Pollution from it, rising upward, made rain clouds. There could be clear blue sky over the swamp, and black clouds, with lightning flashing inside them, over the city towers.

But Ford didn't ever want to go there. He copied Dad's behavior—he tried to pretend the city didn't affect them, even though sometimes Flood Creek stank with the overspill from the city's sewage system. And on days when the pollution levels soared, choking city smog crept along the inlets and made it hard to breathe.

Like Trapper, Ford boasted about the Tuckers' independence: "That city can go to hell for all I care. It's got nothing I need."

Ford watched Gran sluicing down the landing stage. "Is Dad all right?" he asked her finally.

Gran gave him one of her sharp looks. "What do you mean? You think there's something wrong with him?"

Ford shrugged his shoulders. "Dunno. But he's been to check on Hog twice today."

"Has he?" said Gran. She and Ford swapped knowing glances. "Well, you know how jittery he gets when strangers from the city come snooping round."

Ford didn't like Gran using that word *jittery* like Trapper was turning into some kind of nervous wreck. He also didn't like remembering how Dad had really lost it that morning when he'd smashed up the solar panel or the panic and despair he'd seen in Dad's eyes.

"Your dad doesn't like change," Gran was saying as she swilled off the eel slime with another bucket of water. "He wants this place to stay just as it is."

A bell was ringing somewhere deep in the swamp. They hadn't heard it at first because a wailing ambulance siren from the highway had drowned it.

Gran said, "There's Hog."

As soon as he woke up, Hog rang his bell. It meant "I'm hungry, people. Hurry up and feed me."

"He must have slept late today," said Ford. "Lazy old devil." Hog usually rang his bell long before this.

Gran picked up a plastic bag of food scraps, ready and waiting for Hog's summons. There were some sweet potato peelings and the remains of two pork chops, with plenty of meat left on the bone.

The bell tinkled on, faintly, insistently, in the heart of the swamp. Hog wouldn't stop ringing until they got there. But he never had to ring long. Someone always answered his call. It was a Tucker family rule: Never, *ever* keep Hog waiting.

The old dinghy was moored at the landing stage, the one they'd used for eel trapping before Dad bought an expensive new boat.

"You coming?" Gran asked Ford, climbing down into the dinghy.

"Might as well," said Ford, "see how old Hog's doing today."

"I forgot the fork," said Gran. Ford ran to get it. It was a metal toasting fork with a long, long handle. You never knew with Hog. On some days, if he was in an evil mood, you didn't want to get too close when you were feeding him. He had a mean set of teeth.

Firebird looked up from the purse she was making when she heard the dinghy start up. She'd heard Hog's bell, too, and knew where they were going. She clicked her tongue in annoyance. She'd meant to ask Gran for those feathers. Without Gran here, she couldn't get them. Gran kept them locked up in her bedroom cupboard.

Firebird held the purse up to the light, looking at it critically.

Eels are ugly, slimy, snouty, beady-eyed creatures. Most people recoil from them in disgust. No one would believe that something as beautiful and sophisticated as Firebird's purses could be made from their skins. But Firebird had magic fingers. No one had taught her. She just had an eye for color and design.

Even Trapper would comment when Firebird showed him her latest creation. "That girl's got natural talent. Don't know where she gets it from," he'd say, shaking his head in wonder.

Firebird cut and stitched and glued, her fingers busy. But her thoughts were drifting back to what Dr. Pinker had said that morning.

What was all that about? Firebird tried to get it straight in her head.

She said, Firebird reminded herself in shocked amazement, *that the angel came from some old city graveyard. That she got dumped here a hundred years ago.*

If that was true, then the angel hadn't been specially made for Mom at all. She had nothing to do with Mom. She was somebody else's angel.

That thought was too subversive for Firebird to handle. She'd always known the statue as Loreal's angel, never questioned Gran's story about how it came to be in the swamp. But what if Gran's story wasn't true?

Firebird tossed her head scornfully at her own suspicions. She could hardly believe she was thinking this way. Gran's word on family history was never doubted.

That stupid woman was the one who was lying, Firebird insisted to herself. *Never trust strangers. They'll just tell you a pack of lies.*

Firebird would always believe Gran over some stranger from the city.

But a little childish voice in Firebird's head said, *Gran lied about the witch lights. There aren't any witches.*

"Shut up," Firebird told the voice. She was grown-up now. She should know the difference between lies and fairy tales.

Besides, the billboard couldn't lie. And it had been there, rock steady, reliable, marking family events in the little enclosed world of the swamp since before even Gran was born. The day Loreal died, giving birth to Firebird and Ford, there'd been a red Pontiac Firebird on the billboard.

"And there was a big gold pack of cigarettes," Gran always said, "on a dark blue background, the day Trapper brought Loreal's angel here. That packet seemed like a mile high. I remember how it glittered, like a field of ripe corn in the sunshine. And there were two cigarettes sticking out of the top in a *V* shape. And underneath, in black letters on a white background, it said SMOKING KILLS."

How could you argue with facts like those? Firebird could see that ad, from Gran's description, as real as anything in her mind. Like she could see that red Pontiac car that had given her her name.

Course it's Loreal's angel. Course Dad brought her to the swamp, she told herself. How could she have ever doubted it? The billboard had marked it, almost as if it were a witness.

It seemed that all her worries were sorted. So why wouldn't Firebird's mind settle? She wanted to lose herself in making her purse. But for that she needed more feathers.

And they were in that locked cupboard, where Gran also kept all the purses Firebird had ever made.

Firebird had once asked her, "Where do you get the feathers, Gran?" And Gran had said, "Oh, I've had them for years. I used to collect them when I was little. You know, the way kids collect things. They were just lying around in the swamp. Surprising how many feathers birds shed."

But they weren't just ordinary feathers. They were scarlet, golden, vivid metallic blue and green. Firebird had never seen exotic birds like that in the swamp.

But Firebird just wanted to finish her purse. A few more red feathers, that's all she needed. And Gran seemed to have a never-ending supply.

Firebird had never been inside Gran's locked cupboard before. Gran had always been around when she'd wanted feathers. And Firebird never wanted to look at her old purses. When she'd finish one, she'd lose interest. She was already designing the next one in her head.

Would Gran mind? No, decided Firebird, because Gran had been hurrying her to finish this purse, saying, "Finish it today. I can't wait to see it." But her heart was fluttering as she thought, *Where's the key?* She kept looking over her shoulder. Gran hadn't actually said, "Never go into my cupboard when I'm not there." But a little voice in Firebird's head said, *You shouldn't be doing this.*

Firebird had to search around for the key. You'd almost think Gran was hiding it. She finally found it under a white china pot with roses on it. Gran was a formidable woman, one you didn't mess with, but her bedroom was feminine, pink, and frilly.

Thinking only about finishing her purse, Firebird unlocked Gran's cupboard. It was an old oak cupboard, carved with apples and other fruit. It had been in her family, Gran said, for a hundred years. The door swung open. Firebird stared in.

The cupboard was empty. Not empty exactly. There were some folded blankets inside, the spare ones for winter, but there were no feathers anywhere. And no purses wrapped in tissue paper—there should have been a huge pile of those. Firebird lifted the blankets out one by one and shook them to make sure.

No feathers and not a single purse. Her face thoughtful, Firebird folded the blankets up just like they'd been before. She locked the cupboard, put the key back in exactly the same place, so Gran wouldn't know anyone had touched it, and tiptoed out of the bedroom.

6

Down at the bottom of the deep pool, something stirred in the mud. Gran and Ford crouched at the pool's edge, looking in.

"Come on, Hog," said Gran. "We haven't got all day. You wanted feeding, didn't you?"

Something like a ghostly white python came writhing up through the dark water.

"He's coming," said Ford.

Hog's snout broke the surface. His tiny red eyes glared at them.

"You sulking today, Hog?" Ford teased him, while keeping well clear of the pool.

Hog was an albino eel. He wasn't black or brown with a white belly, like all the other eels in the swamp; he was white all over. And it wasn't even a creamy shade of white—it was dead white, like chalk. He was the biggest eel Trapper had ever seen in a lifetime of eel fishing. He was a giant. Hog was as thick as your arm and over a yard and a half long—no one had ever dared stretch him out to measure him. He'd lived in that pool since before Gran was born. Probably sixty years or more, Gran said.

He was called Hog because, like a pig, he ate anything, ripping it apart with his teeth, gnawing chicken carcasses like a dog until he'd rasped off all the meat.

And he was a moody old devil. He'd learned long ago to ring his bell when he needed feeding—the bell rope dangled in the water and Hog tugged it with his teeth when he wanted attention. Sometimes he'd come when you called his name and be like a nice, docile pet, letting you pat his snout and stroke his slimy back. He'd even feed out of your hand. Other times, when he'd snap and thrash the water like a sea monster, you poked the food at him with the toasting fork, let him snatch it off, and he'd plunge back into the depths.

"Oh, he's all right, aren't you, Hog?" said Gran, her freckled arm reaching out to pat his snouty face. Ford held his breath. One bite from those toxic teeth and you'd have an infected wound that wouldn't heal for weeks. But he breathed out again with a long, relieved sigh when Hog nuzzled up to Gran's hand like a friendly puppy.

"You're all right, aren't you, Hog, you old monster," crooned Gran, feeding Hog a pork chop.

Hog never left his pool. He never went slithering through the swamp grass to hunt like other eels. Why should he, when he got fed every day? He just stayed down in the mud, slowly shifting those mighty coils, getting bigger and bigger.

That would be something to see, Ford had often thought: *Hog out on a hunting expedition*. The old heavyweight was big enough to easily take rats and fully grown moorhens. Would even Swamp Dog be safe?

But that could never happen. Hog must never leave his pool. Gran had told them the story, passed down to her by the old eel fishers. So long as Hog stayed in his pool, everything would be fine. The swamp families would ride out any threat. But if Hog moved on, found somewhere else to live, or swam back to the open sea, then the swamp families might as well pack up and leave, too. Because from that time on their luck would be nothing but bad; it would be downhill all the way.

That's why Ford was worried that Dad had been checking on Hog so often lately, as if to reassure himself that Hog was still there and the Tuckers' luck was still holding out. Ford hadn't thought Trapper even *believed* that story about Hog leaving.

"A lot of superstitious garbage," Dad had once scoffed. "Trust your gran to believe it, though. About time I trapped that ugly old eel. He'd fetch a good price at the smokery."

But Dad was only joking. He'd never try to trap Hog. You'd need a giant-sized trap to squeeze him in. And anyway, Hog was too old and wily to fall for it. Not to mention that Gran would have skinned Trapper if he'd tried.

And even if you didn't believe that old story, there was another reason why Hog should stay. He could predict the weather. And that was useful, especially lately when there'd been lots of turbulent weather, lots of sudden freak storms.

Old Hog always knew when there were storms coming, better than any radio or TV forecast. Even deep in his pool, he was in touch with the world outside, as if he could feel the pull of the tides, the wind, the phases of the moon, the changing weather patterns. Trapper said there was no mystical explanation, that Hog just sensed the static electricity in the air that told him there was a storm brewing.

But whatever it was, if Hog's bell rang and it wasn't feeding time, you took refuge in the house, because Flood Creek would soon be rising. Even if the sky was pure blue, you didn't take the boat out because you knew black clouds would soon be massing. Hog was never, ever wrong. Hog's bell had been ringing furiously the night that storm had blown up and drowned Trapper's dad.

Ford was stripping the bark off a willow twig and thinking about what Trapper had done to the solar panel. It was really preying on his mind.

"Gran," he said, "do you think Dad will get into trouble for smashing up that solar panel?"

"Who with, exactly?" asked Gran.

She stopped stroking Hog. He swirled back into the depths, gripping the pork chop between his teeth.

"Those FWS guys," Ford said. "Dad said if they took the swamp over, they'd drive us out."

Gran shook her T-shirt loose and fanned herself with the front of it to get some air to her chest. "It's hot today," she said. She slapped her neck. "And those mosquitoes are worse than ever. You make sure you cover up," she said to Ford.

"Could they, though, Gran?" persisted Ford. "Could they take the swamp over?"

Gran hesitated. And when she spoke, it seemed as if she was choosing her words carefully. "I wouldn't worry about them," she said.

"I'm not!" said Ford, embarrassed that he'd let his fears show too much. "Dad says we'll fight them sooner than let them have it."

"He said *what*?" asked Gran sharply. She shook her head, frowning. "Then he's a bigger fool than I thought."

"No, he's not!" protested Ford. "He's just—"

But he didn't get the chance to finish. "Come on," said Gran brusquely, climbing back into the dinghy. "I can't spend all day here. I've got work to do."

"I'll walk back," said Ford. He was angry and confused that Gran had called Trapper a fool. Didn't she know that he was only trying to stand up for his family, protect what was theirs? Ford would have been disappointed in his dad if he'd done anything else.

Gran shielded her eyes from the sun and squinted up at him. "Suit yourself." She shrugged and started up the outboard.

Ford walked moodily along by Judith's Creek, kicking rocks, deliberately squashing the sundews under his rubber boots. He didn't usually trouble his head with disturbing questions. Nothing much made him fret or worry; he was just happy with the way things were. But even he couldn't ignore it—tension was high between Gran and Trapper. He had the uneasy feeling that there were things they weren't telling him. That made him even angrier—the suspicion that he was being kept in the dark. *What do they think I am? A little kid?* Ford thought resentfully. If it was Firebird they weren't telling, he could understand it—she was in a little world of her own. She just couldn't cope with real life.

Suddenly, a cloud of seagulls rose up, squawking and screaming. They were on the far edge of the swamp, where the creeks all ran into the river.

What are they making such a fuss about? thought Ford.

He wasn't very interested. Seagulls fought over anything: garbage in the river, a rotting fish.

All the same, he made his way in that direction, plunging through the twisty tunnels in the reeds. He didn't have anything else to do until Dad came back from the smokery. If he went back home now, Gran would only find him some extra chores.

As he got nearer to the wide, slow-flowing river, the swamp opened out and became less dense and tangled. The city towers still gleamed behind him, a constant presence. But they seemed much farther away, not so looming. The traffic roar was muffled, too. Sometimes, when he came down here, Ford even imagined he could smell the salty tang of the distant ocean.

You often saw tankers and other big boats sliding down the brown, muddy river to the ocean. But Ford wasn't looking out for tankers now. Those seagulls were still squabbling, just offshore, yelping and snapping at each other like a pack of dogs.

Ford crouched in the reeds. He didn't have anything to

hide from in particular, but it came naturally to the Tuckers to keep to themselves. Their family motto, if they'd had one, would have been "Mind your own business." These days, though, that seemed to be getting harder and harder.

Who was at the center of that noisy scrap? Ford strained his eyes to see. It was just someone in a boat, some fisherman, and the gulls were probably after his bait. Ford was about to turn away—nothing interesting there. But then some of the gulls swirled off and he got a clearer view.

"Dad!" muttered Ford. "What's he doing there?" He should have been at the smokery by now.

Ford almost leaped up, waved, and shouted, "Dad! Dad!" Not that Trapper would have heard him—he was too far away from the shore. But then Ford saw what Trapper was doing. His eyes widened in disbelief. Trapper was tipping the boxes of eels they'd caught that morning, one by one, into the river. That's what the seagulls were diving for and fighting over.

Ford stared, bewildered. "He can't be!" But there was no mistake. There went another box, emptied into the water. That was all their hard work wasted. There was nothing wrong with those eels. And what about all the money Dad would have gotten for them? Eels were fetching top prices right now. Dad had said so.

Ford just couldn't understand it. It didn't make any sense. Except, now he remembered, Gran hadn't wanted any ice, as if she hadn't expected Trapper to be going far with the eels, as if it didn't even matter whether they kept fresh or not.

What's going on here? It was the scared child inside him

that asked that question. Not the tough, button-lipped Ford who did a man's job, working alongside Trapper.

What's going on? that scared child repeated, in a lost and helpless voice.

And instead of jumping up, yelling to attract Dad's attention, Ford crouched down even lower and scurried away through the reeds, feeling he'd seen things he shouldn't have.

7

FIREBIRD was already making excuses for Gran.

Perhaps she put the purses and feathers somewhere else, she was telling herself. But she couldn't think where. This wasn't a big house. All those purses would take up a lot of space. And she'd already looked everywhere they could possibly be, even in Trapper's bedroom.

Firebird wanted to know where they'd gone. But when Gran came back from feeding Hog, Firebird found herself being guarded. She didn't ask straight out; she had the uneasy feeling that she'd done something wrong, unlocking Gran's cupboard and looking inside.

"I can't finish my purse," said Firebird, holding it up to show Gran so that it shimmered in the light. "I need some more feathers."

"The purse's fine," said Gran. "It's beautiful. It looks finished to me. Give it here and I'll put it in my cupboard, with all the others." She heaved herself out of her chair. "Phew," she said, "it's hot."

Firebird watched, her face grave, her eyes accusing, as Gran wrapped the purse in tissue paper and went into the bedroom. "Yep," said Gran, opening the cupboard, putting it in, "I've got a real collection in here."

Oh yeah? thought Firebird.

"But you know how I like to collect things."

"Like the feathers," murmured Firebird to herself.

Gran had already locked the cupboard. She walked past Firebird to make herself a drink in the kitchen. Firebird's eyes bored into her back.

Gran must have wondered why Firebird was so strangely silent. Why her gaze was so suspicious. Gran tried to be chatty. "Want some juice?" she asked Firebird. "I'm having some." Then she added, as if she'd just thought of it, "Oh, I forgot to get you more feathers out of the cupboard. I've locked it up now. I'll give 'em to you tomorrow, when you start a new purse."

Gran came back and stood behind Firebird. Firebird turned her head away not making eye contact. "Is anything the matter?" asked Gran.

Slowly, Firebird shook her head.

"Come for a cuddle," said Gran, folding Firebird in her big brawny arms. "That purse you just finished, it was your best yet."

Firebird held herself stiff, totally unyielding. She was as prickly as a porcupine, warning: don't come near.

Then suddenly, Gran launched into one of the old stories that Firebird loved so much. The ones about when Gran was a little girl and the billboard.

"Those red feathers," said Gran, "they reminded me.

They were just the same color as those shoes I wanted so much."

Firebird let her guard down; her face softened. She hadn't meant it to, but she just couldn't help it. She was a sucker for those old swamp stories, especially when they featured the billboard.

"I remember the day they put up the poster," said Gran. "I must have only been about five or six. And after they'd gone, I sneaked round to the other side of the billboard to see it. I spent hours just sitting and staring at it. And there was this family, Mom, Dad, and two kids, all smiling with big, white teeth, all dressed in their best clothes. The kids had scrubbed rosy cheeks and curly blond hair. They were so cute—they were just perfect. I'm telling you." Gran chuckled. "They didn't look anything like us swamp kids."

And Firebird smiled, too, imagining the barefoot, muddy swamp kids and the squeaky-clean, perfect family up on the billboard.

"And over their heads it said in big letters, WHY DON'T YOU WORSHIP TOGETHER THIS SUNDAY? So they must've been going to church. But it was the little girl's shoes that I liked. I kept going back to look at them, over and over again."

"The red leather shoes," murmured Firebird, who couldn't stop herself from joining in the story, "with a crossover strap and a red button."

"That's right," said Gran, her hand stealing back onto Firebird's shoulder. "I wanted those shoes more than anything. I mean, I didn't have a hope in hell of getting them;

it was a bad time for eel fishing then. But I wanted them so much it hurt."

Firebird nodded in sympathy; she knew that feeling. The ad on the billboard now made her heart ache with longing—those snowy mountains, those sandy beaches, places no daughter of Loreal would ever see. Because she had to stay in the swamp—forever.

Gran knew, when she saw Firebird's stony face melt, that she'd won her over, just like she always did with her billboard stories. But then she made a big mistake. She added a bit to the story, suddenly, impulsively, as if she was giving Firebird a present for being a good, cooperative girl.

"And I don't think I've ever told you this bit," said Gran. "I wanted those shoes that little girl was wearing so badly—I mean, I'd never wanted anything so much in my whole life—that when the guys came to take the poster down I went and spoke to them. They said, 'Who are you?' And I told 'em, 'I'm Carol-Ann Tucker.'"

"You didn't!" exclaimed Firebird, who appreciated what a dangerous and reckless thing this was to do. Even now, Trapper was always saying, "Never, ever give any information about yourself to strangers."

"Anyway," said Gran, "you know how they tear the old posters off the billboard? Just rip them off in pieces? Well, I pleaded with them to give me that one little piece with the red shoes."

Firebird, completely captivated now, turned to look at Gran. "And did they?" she asked eagerly.

Gran nodded. "They did. This guy, he peeled that

piece off really carefully and he ʌ
Carol-Ann Tucker.'"

"So what did you do with it?" asked
ture of the red shoes?"

Gran laughed. She seemed captivated b.
"Well, I slept with it under my pillow for a w.
I sort of lost interest in the shoes. Maybe thei ͺne-
thing else up on the billboard I liked better. But ι kept that
little piece of poster a long, long time. I had it in my old
cupboard, where I keep the purses and feathers now . . ."

In an instant, the spell of the red-shoe story was broken. Firebird felt as if a bucket of freezing water had been
thrown in her face.

She leaped up from the table so abruptly that she sent
her chair flying. She went rushing out of the house.

Gran looked after her and shook her head, bewildered.
Firebird was usually so placid, no trouble at all.

FIREBIRD sat in the swamp, in another of her hidey-holes,
an inlet off Whiskey Creek. Next to her was a boggy patch
of sundews, glowing like rubies, flies trapped in their sticky
strands. Behind her, a bloodred sun was setting over the
city, making its glass towers blaze as if they were on fire. It
was rush hour. The traffic roar was thunderous, the gasoline stink sickening. Out on the lonely reed beds by the
river, a heron squawked. But Firebird wasn't aware of any
of that. She was thinking, trying to sort things out in her
head.

The rushes quivered. Firebird looked up. Was it

og? No, it was Ford, plonking himself down be-
her.

"I've been looking for you," he said. "I looked by Mom's angel and the other side of the billboard. Everywhere."

Firebird wondered why he'd been trying to find her. She and Ford were twins, but that hadn't made them close or given them any secret bond. They were too different. They never had much to say to each other. In her heart, Firebird thought her brother was boring, and not too bright. His whole life was eel trapping; he didn't seem to want anything else.

"Why? Does Gran want me?" she asked him.

But Ford didn't answer. He just stayed silent as the grave, sitting tight-lipped beside her. But his fingers were busy, making a daisy chain out of the pink marsh flowers. Then, as if he'd caught himself doing something shamefully childish, he chucked it into the water. It went twirling off down the creek.

As if the words were being dragged out of him, Ford finally said, "Dad dumped the eels."

"What?" said Firebird.

"Dad didn't go to the smokery like he said. He dumped the eels in the river."

"Are you sure?"

"I saw him."

Firebird shrugged. "He probably had a good reason."

Ford nodded, gratefully. "That's what I thought, too."

"Have you asked him?" said Firebird.

"No," said Ford. "He isn't back yet. But I will."

Ford started to get up, as if the conversation was over,

the subject settled. But Firebird wasn't finished. Suddenly, she heard herself saying, "I looked in Gran's cupboard." She hadn't meant to share her worries with Ford, but who else was there to tell? She now had in the back of her mind a nagging suspicion that Trapper and Gran were somehow colluding, keeping secrets from them. What secrets? Firebird wasn't even sure. And she knew she could be dead wrong. She got carried away sometimes. Her imagination dreamed up the craziest things.

Ford shrugged and said, "What do you mean, you looked in Gran's cupboard? Big deal." He thought Firebird's affairs, with her eel-skin purses and feathers, were girlie and trivial compared to what he did, working alongside Trapper, earning money, supporting the family.

"The cupboard just had blankets in it," said Firebird. "She doesn't keep my purses in there, like she said. There weren't any feathers, either."

"So?" said Ford. "What's the problem? She probably put them somewhere else."

"She didn't," Firebird blurted out. "I looked everywhere. And she even *pretended* they were in there, when I knew they weren't. She told me lies, right to my face."

Now she'd said that, something she'd hardly dared admit to herself, other things poured out of Firebird's mouth. "I met this woman, Dr. Pinker, this morning near Mom's angel. She said the angel isn't Mom's memorial at all. That it's been here a hundred years. That it came from some old city graveyard . . ."

Ford stared at her in astonishment. "A hundred years?" he repeated slowly.

But his mind was already rejecting what Firebird had said. Ford didn't want anything to rock his little swamp world. He just couldn't cope with that.

"You'll believe anything, won't you?" he scoffed at Firebird. "Remember what Dad said? Never trust strangers. They just tell you lies."

"But why?" asked Firebird. "Why would Dr. Pinker lie about the angel?"

Ford shook his head and waved his arms around as if wasps were attacking him. "I don't know why. But what she said, it's a load of crap. And she shouldn't be sneaking around here anyway. She'll be sorry, if Dad catches her."

Ford jumped up. That settled that, as far as he was concerned. And Trapper dumping the eels—that was settled, too. Firebird had reassured him, had said just what he wanted to hear. That Trapper must have his reasons.

Course he had, thought Ford, his faith in Trapper restored. *Maybe I won't even bother to ask him.*

"Don't ever listen to strangers," Ford warned Firebird, sounding just like Dad. "They always tell you lies. See you later," he said, plunging back into the reeds.

Firebird gazed after her brother. She wished she could keep things as simple as Ford did, see things in black and white. Gran always told her, "You think too much. Too much thinking's bad for you."

But a little sneaking voice in her head kept saying, *Gran isn't a stranger, she's family.* Yet she lied about what was in the cupboard. How could you explain that away? No purses, no feathers. Maybe there'd never been any picture of red shoes, either. Maybe that whole red-shoe story was a load of lies and that billboard ad had never even existed. Like that cigarette ad the day Dad brought Loreal's angel to the swamp—because Dad never did bring the angel to the swamp, because according to Dr. Pinker it was already here . . .

Shut up! Shut up! Firebird told herself.

There she went again, running out of control, thinking the most outrageous things. Gran wouldn't lie about the ads on the billboard or about Mom's memorial. Course she wouldn't.

Firebird wrapped her arms around her body, hugging herself. "I'm so mixed up," she moaned. She didn't know what was true anymore, what was made up and what had really happened. "I don't want to think about it. I don't want to think about it," she chanted, trying to block out those shocking thoughts. She wished she'd never met Dr. Linda Pinker or unlocked Gran's cupboard.

Firebird rocked herself to and fro for comfort. The little sundew plants lured more gnats to a sticky death. Behind her, in the gathering dark beyond the billboard, an ambulance rushed off to some emergency with its siren wailing.

WHILE Firebird rocked herself, Trapper was seeking reassurance of his own. He hadn't gone home. Instead, he'd gotten a beer from the cooler on the boat and was sitting by Hog's pool, drinking it.

Trapper tipped back his head and took a long pull from the beer can. He was under a lot of stress—trying to pretend to Ford and Firebird that everything was going fine, when he felt that things were falling apart.

"There you are, you old devil," said Trapper fondly. He could see a squirming white stain down in the inky blackness. He raised his beer can to Hog in a mock salute. "Least you're still here," he said.

Trapper had stopped believing that story long ago, the one his mom had told him when he was growing up, just like she told her grandchildren, Ford and Firebird, now. About how Hog was some kind of guardian of the swamp. And how, when the great white eel left, the swamp would be finished. Trapper hadn't believed that for years. So he hardly knew why, just lately, he'd been coming to check on Hog two or even three times a day. Just to make sure he hadn't deserted them. Trapper sneered at himself for doing it. *You're turning into a kid again.* But he still kept coming.

Hog was restless tonight, moving around, stirring up clouds of mud. He hadn't rung his bell yet. But Trapper wondered if there was bad weather coming.

Trapper shivered. He'd been doing a lot of that lately, his body feeling feverish, then cold and clammy. He took another swig from his beer can.

"Don't you go running out on us," he said, while down in the dark pool, Hog's ghostly coils writhed.

8

FORD wasn't mixed up at all. Or at least, that's what he tried to tell himself.

He hung around, waiting for Trapper to come home, but when he didn't show up Ford went to bed. He'd already decided not to ask Dad about dumping the eels. Not because he was worried about finding out things he didn't want to know, but because he trusted Dad. It wasn't cool to fuss and pester Dad with stupid questions, to be needy—that's the way little kids behaved. There was an understanding, a bond, between him and Dad. They didn't need words. If Trapper thought Ford ought to know something, he'd tell him.

So, with everything sorted out in his own mind, Ford fell asleep.

In her own room, Firebird was lying in bed, her eyes wide open, staring at the ceiling. Nothing could slow her racing mind. Angels' faces, purses, feathers, and red shoes swirled around in her head. Usually, pretending the traffic's roar was ocean waves would send her drifting off to sleep, like a lullaby. But this time even that didn't work.

Suddenly, Firebird sat up in bed. She'd heard a noise downstairs. It was the sound of the back door closing.

It was Gran, going out on one of her nighttime rambles.

Gran used to have no trouble sleeping. Like Ford and Trapper, she did hard physical work all day. She used to say, "As soon as my head touches that pillow, I'm out like a light."

But since last year it had all been different. "Some nights I just can't drop off," she'd say. And when sleep wouldn't come, she'd go outside, sometimes for hours.

"What do you *do* out there?" Firebird had once asked her.

"Oh." Gran had shrugged, as if it was no big deal, "Nothing special. I just sit on the landing stage and watch the swamp by moonlight until I feel sleepy."

Firebird sighed, slumped down in her hot, sweaty bed, closed her eyes, and tried again to make sleep come. A bright moonbeam slanted across her pillow. She could see it even behind her eyelids. She groaned and got up to close the gap in her curtains. She expected to see Gran, sitting hunched on the landing stage, watching the fireflies.

Gran wasn't there. But, even though her mind was swarming with new suspicions, Firebird wasn't alarmed.

"If I'm not on the landing stage," Gran had once told her, "don't be worried. I sometimes take a little stroll in the swamp, sit awhile by your mom's memorial."

At night, the city lights and moonlight made the

swamp a magical, spooky place—a hazy mix of eerie, glowing light and shadow.

Firebird yawned. She was about to stumble back to bed—she felt she might sleep now—but then she spotted Gran, in her usual baggy jeans and T-shirt. But Gran wasn't going to sit by Mom's memorial. She was heading the other way, with that brisk, purposeful stride of hers. And she was wearing a backpack.

Where's she going? thought Firebird, instantly alert. She didn't have a clear view now. Gran was hidden by willow trees.

That direction only led to the billboard. Through a gap in the willows, Firebird caught sight of Gran again. She was heading straight for the back of the billboard. It towered over her, a mighty gray wall. Firebird just took it for granted that she would stop there. Where else was there to go?

But Gran didn't stop, or turn back. Instead, to Firebird's astonishment, she squeezed under the billboard, using the same tunnel through the weeds and spiky bushes that Firebird used when she paid a visit to the other side.

Is that what Gran was up to? Billboard gazing? Firebird felt resentful, as if the billboard spoke to her alone.

"Maybe she's up to something else," muttered Firebird, her voice prickly with suspicion. She dragged on her clothes and shoes and slipped out of the house to follow Gran.

Outside, the swamp seemed almost peaceful in the moonlight. In a brief lull in the traffic's noise, Firebird could hear frogs croaking in secret, hidden pools.

Firebird hurried after Gran, across the yard, along a twisty path through the reeds. She wriggled like a snake under the billboard, scrambled to her feet, expecting Gran to be sitting there, in *her* spot, staring at *her* poster.

But Gran wasn't there. So where was she?

Firebird gazed up at the billboard looming above her, as if for help and inspiration. But its message, LIVE YOUR DREAMS! and those pictures of faraway paradises were shrouded in darkness.

Dismayed, Firebird turned her back on the billboard and looked the other way. Bleak scrubland sloped down to the highway. Even now, cars sped by, their lights yellow blurs in the night. Then there was the city, a glowing sprawl on the landscape.

Firebird felt exposed, standing there beyond the billboard. When she wriggled through to see the ads, she never stood upright like this; she'd just crouch, hidden in the grass. She shivered, hugged herself, and stared unhappily about.

Then she saw Gran, striding down through the scrubland, toward the highway.

Follow her, a voice in Firebird's head whispered. While another said, *Go back to bed. Mind your own business.* She'd have to decide right now. Gran was getting away.

Then Firebird felt a cold nose slide into her hand.

Swamp Dog. What was he doing beyond the billboard? She stroked his narrow, lizardlike head. But he shook free, and began trotting down through the scrubland confidently, as if he knew the way. Then he stopped and looked back, as if he were waiting for her.

Firebird took one last longing look at the billboard. But it had no help to offer—she had to decide for herself. Slowly, she moved away from its shelter and protection, away from the swamp where she'd spent all her life. She felt a queasy cramping in the pit of her stomach. But it wasn't just fear that was making her feel sick. There was another emotion churning inside her. It was excitement.

She'd made up her mind. Firebird took a deep, shaky breath and plunged into the scrubland, following Gran and Swamp Dog toward the city.

9

FIREBIRD could see Gran striding ahead of her, a black moving shape against a paler night sky. Firebird followed her. She didn't have to fight through scratchy bushes. There was a path, twisting down through the scrubland, as though someone had been this way many times before.

The highway was just below them, blazing with lights, roaring with traffic. Was Gran going to try and cross it and dodge those monster trucks?

But she swerved to the right and stayed in the dark. Then Firebird lost sight of her.

Where's she gone? was her instant, panicky reaction. She stopped, looked around, bewildered. She thought she'd lost Swamp Dog, too. Then heard him whine softly, somewhere ahead of her. She hurried along the path to find him.

Suddenly, the path and scrubland ran out. Firebird stared about her, wide-eyed. Where was she?

Then she looked up and figured it out. She was under the overpass. It soared above her and the great concrete columns supporting it were all around. It was a creepy place, lit only by stray moonbeams and headlight flashes. Down here, the traffic noise echoed like thunder.

Firebird crept among the concrete pillars. All at once the ground shook. Firebird clung to a pillar. But it was only a subway train, deep underground.

"Sh—" Firebird bit off her startled curse, in case Gran heard. She'd almost fallen into a deep, wide trench. She kneeled down to peer into it. It was a storm drain, concrete-lined, built to stop the city from flooding. There was debris in it, sticks and garbage, washed here from last time the river burst its banks.

Firebird suddenly shrank back into the shadows. She'd seen Gran. She was down in the storm drain, walking along it.

Firebird dropped down into the drain, too. Immediately, she thought better of it, but she was stuck down there now. The sides came up higher than her head, so she couldn't see out. She couldn't climb out, either. She was down too deep and the concrete sides were too smooth and slimy. All she could do was follow Gran, and hope she knew where she was going.

Firebird stumbled along the drain in the flickering gloom, terrified of losing her. Terrified, too, that Gran would turn around and say, "Firebird! Are you spying on me?" But Gran didn't once look back, as if being followed never crossed her mind.

At least the drain was almost empty, just a few scummy puddles on the bottom. But it was hard going, dark and slippery. A tree blocked her way, wedged in the drain. She had to wriggle through its white, dead branches. And all the time she was thinking, *You shouldn't be here.* The excitement she felt when she'd started out was gone now. She just wanted to be safe, back behind the billboard.

She should have stayed in the swamp, where she belonged. Been a home-lover like Mom, listened to Dad's warnings. Beyond the billboard was an ugly, scary place to be.

She almost got left behind when Gran turned right into another storm drain. There were moments of heart-stopping panic as Firebird backtracked to find her.

When Firebird caught up with her, Gran was climbing some slimy concrete steps. *She knows the way out of here,* thought Firebird with a deep, thankful sigh. She thought they'd be trapped in these drains forever.

Firebird hung back a while until Gran reached the top step, then disappeared. She felt a squirming around her legs.

"Swamp Dog. Where've you been, boy?" she whispered, crouching down to stroke him. The air down here was thick and polluted. Firebird tasted gasoline with every breath she took. Swamp Dog smelled pungently of swamp— of mud and weed and dead crabs. But Firebird sniffed his coat as if it were the most expensive perfume.

He pulled away from her and trotted confidently up the steps after Gran, as if he knew the way out of the drains, too. Firebird rushed after him. Gran was getting too far ahead. And she was terrified of being left behind.

They were in an old white-tiled tunnel lit by blurred yellow lights. It was part of a system of old underground walkways meant for pedestrians. But few people used these scary, stinking passages now. Or even knew they existed.

Gran was still charging ahead with that determined stride. Firebird was concentrating on keeping that green, bobbing backpack in sight. But then her foot hit something. She looked down. On the white-tiled floor was a heap of rags. It moved, groaned.

Firebird hurried on, not daring to look back. Where was Gran? There! There she was! Firebird almost sobbed with relief. Gran was climbing a long stairway to the surface.

"Keep back," Firebird hissed at Swamp Dog, "so she doesn't see us."

But Gran still didn't turn around, as if she'd crossed over into another world and left the swamp and her family far behind.

Firebird and Swamp Dog popped up from underground into a dazzle of steel, glass, and lights.

Firebird stood, fixed to the spot, dazed and confused by the glare. Glass walls soared around her, glittering blue and black. Her eyes traveled dizzily up them, her mouth hanging open. They seemed to go on forever. She had to throw her head back to see their tops.

Then, to her amazement, she saw something familiar. Coming from the top of the tallest, proudest tower was that circling light. The one that, every night, raked the sky over the city with its brilliant beam.

We can see that from the swamp, thought Firebird, somehow feeling a little less of a stranger.

Then her eyes traveled back downward. A sign read: CENTRAL PLAZA.

"I'm in the city," murmured Firebird in a stunned whisper.

She took in the plaza's wide-open, traffic-free spaces. Lights all around made it seem as bright as day. She saw benches on blue-tile pavements, fountains splashing water, shiny steel sculptures, and blossom trees.

Despite herself, she was entranced. Why had no one told her that the city was this beautiful?

Firebird ventured a few steps. She knew she needed to find Gran instead of staring around in a dream. Boldly, she walked out onto the plaza's blue tiles with Swamp Dog cringing beside her.

But where are all the people? she wondered. Firebird thought she might see Dr. Pinker. She came from the city, didn't she?

But there was no Dr. Pinker, no people at all. The plaza was eerily still—its shops and restaurants shut up, its offices empty.

Firebird almost called out "Gran? Where are you?" not even caring if Gran found out she'd been followed.

Then she breathed easily again. It was all right. There was Gran at the other side of the plaza. What was she doing? She'd stopped in front of a shop, its window lit up, a yellow square of light. She'd taken a parcel out of her backpack and slid it through the mail slot. Then she moved away. There were some tables with striped umbrellas left outside a café at the far corner of the plaza. Gran plonked herself down on one of the spindly iron chairs. Firebird could see a red tip glowing.

"She's having a smoke," whispered Firebird to Swamp Dog. Gran wasn't even looking their way. Just gazing into the distance, in a smoke-ringed trance.

Firebird and Swamp Dog crept around the plaza, keeping close to the buildings. Firebird wanted to look into that shop window. When she reached it, a fountain hid her from Gran's view. Which was good, for Firebird stared, helplessly lost in wonder, her nose pressed against the glass.

"My purses," she breathed.

There were just three of them for sale in the window, displayed on velvet, as if they were precious objects. There was the one she'd made last week, the eel skin supple and silvery with dappled markings. The feathers Gran had given her to decorate that purse had been extra beautiful—golden, green, iridescent.

Firebird's eyes gobbled up details. The words on the labels: *handmade, an investment, must-have accessory, each one unique*. And the prices! Firebird gasped, shook her head in disbelief. All that money—as much as the wad of bills Trapper brought back each week from the smokery.

Firebird thought, *This can't be true. I'm dreaming.*

Then she heard an iron chair scraping. Gran was on the move again.

Firebird tore herself away from the window, crouched behind the fountain, and peered over the rim, water droplets sprinkling her hair.

A hundred different thoughts were howling at her, like

a wolf pack inside her head. She tried to beat them down, to get back in control. But one kept leaping up at her: *Gran, you were lying to me all along.*

Firebird knew now where her purses ended up. Not in a locked cupboard, but in a fancy shop where they were sold for breathtaking sums of money. She was sure that Gran had just delivered her latest purse.

Over by the black granite columns of an international bank, Gran was picking something off the floor. It was vivid orange. She stashed it carefully in her backpack.

An orange rind? thought Firebird. *What's she want that for?* Was it food scraps for Hog? He'd eat anything.

And at the same time, down by her sneakers, she saw Swamp Dog sniffing at a dog turd on the blue tiles.

Only it wasn't a dog turd. It was a pathetic bundle of brown feathers, a dead bird.

And now Firebird, as she peeped over the rim of the fountain, could see other bird corpses littering the plaza, birds with brightly colored plumage: tanagers, orioles, hummingbirds, parakeets. She should have noticed them before. But her mind had been dazzled by so many new sights and new sensations.

Who killed them? thought Firebird. *What are they doing here, anyway?* Birds like that didn't live here. They just flew overhead on their usual migration routes, south in winter, north in summer.

Gran was scooping up their bodies like fallen fruit, stuffing them into her backpack. She darted over to a golden oriole. Even dead, its feathers gleamed.

So this is where she gets my feathers from, thought Firebird. *All that crap about collecting them in the swamp when she was a little girl. Why did she tell me that?*

But Firebird already knew why. Tuckers weren't supposed to come to the city. It was strictly off-limits. "That city's got nothing we need," Dad boasted. How many times had Firebird heard him say that?

Gran was moving closer. Firebird ducked lower, behind the fountain. Gran was very near now. Firebird could almost have reached out and touched her. Gran had no idea she was being watched. She was too absorbed in her feather hunt.

Firebird saw her pick up a ruby-throated hummingbird that was still fluttering feebly. It was hopelessly damaged, with only one wing.

With a quick flick of her thumb, Gran snapped its neck, as casually as she whopped eels on the landing stage. She stuffed it into her backpack.

Firebird shuddered, even though she knew the bird couldn't survive—it was kinder to end its suffering.

Now Gran had darted away, pouncing on another prize at the other end of the plaza. Swamp Dog whimpered. "Shhhh," warned Firebird, looking down.

Then she saw that the sad scrap of feathers Swamp Dog had been sniffing at was alive, too. Its claws were clenching and unclenching. Its eyes, two tiny black beads, opened. Firebird didn't know what kind of bird it was. It was brown, but on its chest was a splash of brilliant blue.

By some miracle, the bird didn't seem damaged, just dazed. It fluttered to its feet, rocked, made little fluttering hops out into the plaza.

No, you don't, thought Firebird. Gently, she cupped her hand over it and closed her fingers.

All the other thoughts in her head were eclipsed. Just one shone out. *Set it free.* Somewhere away from the plaza. What if Gran found it? Maybe she wouldn't notice it still had a chance of life. Maybe all she'd see was its brilliant blue feathers and think, *Wow. That'd make a really nice purse.*

Instinctively, Firebird looked around for green. But only tall glass towers crowded around her. The sky was just a strip, impossibly distant. Then, at the end of a street, she saw a frizz of green. Were they trees? She set off in that direction in a crouching run, Swamp Dog racing after her.

Nothing seemed more important at that moment than the tiny bird she was carrying. It was so light it felt like her hand held nothing but air. Had it somehow slipped through her fingers? She stopped running, opened her hand to check. It was still curled in her palm, its eyes bright, its beak open. She set off again. And now she could feel its tiny heartbeat quivering against her fingers.

There were people in this street. Someone stared. Someone called out, "Hey, little girl!" But Firebird sprinted past.

At last, she skidded to a halt. She'd left the skyscrapers behind. She was in a tiny park, a little oasis of benches, trees, and flowers. She could see the sky overhead, or at least a bigger patch of it. She opened her fingers and held her hand palm up like a launching pad.

The bird flew away from the city. A single blue flash and it was gone, on its long migration journey.

Firebird was left down below, trembling and panting from her run, all alone in the middle of the city.

She couldn't remember the way back to the plaza. Panic-stricken, she gazed around. Then, on a post, she saw signs pointing off in all directions: CITY HOSPITAL. TRAIN STATION. LIBRARY. CENTRAL PLAZA.

She raced back to the plaza with Swamp Dog, hurling herself into the open space. She didn't even care if Gran saw her.

But Gran wasn't there. Wildly, Firebird crisscrossed the plaza, searching every corner and among the café tables. Twice she passed the fancy shop where her purses were displayed but didn't even glance in the window.

"She's gone," said Firebird to Swamp Dog, her voice filled with dread and disbelief.

She whirled around and shrank back into a restaurant doorway. A little yellow machine with a man on it came whirring into the plaza. It was street cleaning, scraping chewing gum off the tiles, vacuuming up litter. All the bird bodies Gran hadn't picked up were sucked inside it so the people in daytime never saw them—never knew about the nighttime carnage or the bird corpses in their plaza. The machine trundled off, down a side street.

Firebird came out from her hiding place and spun around. Panic made her dizzy and disoriented. The harsh lights, the reflections from glass, steel, and glistening marble hurt her eyes. She couldn't tell where she'd come into the plaza or how to get back down into the tunnel. She saw green and instinctively plunged toward it and smashed into glass. An artificial tree gleamed inside the lobby of the tallest tower.

"Where are you going?" she shouted after Swamp Dog as he scooted off. Surely he wasn't abandoning her, too? Then at last, reason kicked in. *Maybe he knows the way back.*

Dad always said he'd been a city dog. "Couldn't stand it there anymore," Trapper said. "That's why he moved to the swamp."

"Here, boy!" Firebird ran after the scurrying Swamp Dog. He knew the way all right; he'd found the subway entrance. She saw his narrow haunches wriggling down the stairway. She clattered down after him. Now she was back in that creepy, white-tiled tunnel that stretched away into the distance. But she felt safer somehow, as if she'd escaped from the city. Swamp Dog had stopped racing ahead. He sniffed the air, suddenly starting to whine and shake.

"What's up, boy?" said Firebird, her voice echoing eerily.

Another voice came out of the dark. "That's my dog," it growled. "Where'd you find him?"

Firebird whipped around. A man, big, bearded, and smelly, had crept out of an unlit side tunnel. "Where'd you find that dog?" he said again. "He's mine."

He aimed a kick at Swamp Dog with his heavy boots. "Teach you to run away from me."

Swamp Dog took off like a rocket, his claws skittering on the tile floor. The man didn't move out of Firebird's way. Instead, he lurched closer, pressing against her.

"You're pretty," he said. His eyes were blue slits in a beaten-up, weathered face. His breathing was heavy. Firebird dodged under his elbow and ran like demons were after her. She could hear his voice echoing down the tunnel, "Hey, come back here. I'm not going to hurt you! I just want to talk."

Firebird ran until she had to stop, doubled over and gasping because of the stabbing pain in her side. It lessened, at least enough for her to stand up. Fearfully, she looked back down the subway. There was no one following, no one even in sight. Then she felt a touch on her leg. Her heart gave a sick lurch. She almost threw up. Trembling, she looked down.

"Swamp Dog." He'd waited for her. She leaned against the greasy wall, dizzy with relief.

Swamp Dog led her back, out of the tunnels, down the concrete steps into the storm-drain system. Firebird's nerves were in shreds. She kept looking behind her. She wondered where Gran was. She thought, *How am I going to get out of this drain?*

Swamp Dog showed her how. When they came to a dead tree, he used it as a ladder, scrambling up its branches and leaping out of the drain like a flying squirrel. Now he was looking back down, barking encouragement to her.

Firebird climbed up the same way and jumped across. She managed to give Swamp Dog a shaky grin. "Why didn't I think of that?"

When they came out from under the overpass, Firebird lifted her eyes to the billboard. The sky behind it was lightening now, streaked with pink. She could see its message, fuzzily emerging from the murk: "LIVE YOUR DREAMS!" But she hardly glanced at it; it didn't lift her spirits. Firebird mistrusted even the billboard now, as if it was part of the web of lies she was caught in.

She lowered her eyes and trudged through the scrubland after Swamp Dog.

She felt she should be doing some hard thinking, trying to understand what she'd seen in the city. But her mind was too weary, too numb to think about anything at all.

Firebird had one picture in her mind. It was of the bird, light as a dandelion seed, that she'd held in her hand. And that flash of blue when she'd opened her fingers and watched it fly to freedom.

She crawled under the billboard. Swamp Dog shot off into the swamp, on some business of his own. Firebird trailed through the yard. She guessed that Gran had got home before her and gone to bed. The boat was still moored at the landing stage. That meant Dad and Ford hadn't gone out to check eel traps yet—with any luck they'd still be in bed, too. Firebird, swaying with weariness, slipped into the quiet house unseen, and went to her room.

But only a few seconds later, it seemed, Gran was shaking her awake.

"Get up," she said. "Your dad's sick."

She'd meant to make a fresh start this morning, confront Gran and tell her, "I followed you last night. I know where you get the feathers from, what you do with my purses. Why did you tell me all those lies?"

She'd even meant to demand the truth about Loreal's angel.

But Dad being sick somehow made everything different. And, besides that, Firebird suddenly felt scared. As if letting on that she knew the family's secrets would be like opening Pandora's box, bringing down death and destruction on all their heads.

"What are you looking so long-faced about?" Gran asked her. "We need cheery faces around here."

"I-I," stuttered Firebird. Hog's bell saved her. Its shrill command tinkled above the traffic drone. He was saying, "I need food. *Now*."

"You'll have to wait, you old devil," muttered Gran.

"No," said Trapper, his teeth chattering. "Feed him. If we make him wait, he might . . ."

"Leave the swamp?" said Gran with a scornful roll of her eyes. "You don't believe *that* old fairy tale, do you, Trapper?"

"We have to feed him *now*," insisted Trapper. "Firebird can go."

"Fine, fine," Gran sighed, as if she was soothing a fretful child.

She flapped her hand at Firebird. "You'd better do what your dad says." She gave Firebird a secret glance that said, *You can see the mood he's in.* Then she frowned. "What can we feed old Hog? Wait a minute."

She hurried off into the kitchen. Dad sat brooding, shivering, staring into the fire. Firebird knew that all the questions she'd meant to ask would have to wait until later.

Gran came back and thrust a blue plastic box at Firebird. "He'll have to make do with that," she said. Hog's bell was ringing even more urgently.

"Aren't you gone yet?" said Trapper.

"And when you come back," said Gran, "how about starting another purse? I've found some great feathers in my collection. Forgot I had them. Ruby-colored . . ."

Gran stopped. She'd thought Firebird would say, "Oh, great!" But Firebird's eyes met hers with a cold, cynical gaze.

"What are you looking at me like that for?" said Gran, startled. "Don't you dare look at me like that."

Firebird dropped her eyes. But Gran was angry now, muttering, "You'd better go back to bed when you get back, sleep off that bad mood."

"Leave the girl alone," said Trapper feebly.

Firebird whirled around and went rushing out through the kitchen.

"Everybody's in a bad mood today," muttered Gran.

Firebird snatched some bread to chew on her way to feed Hog and headed into the yard. The first thing she saw were the city's towers, soaring above the billboard. And above even them rose the tallest, the searchlight beam on its roof switched off during daylight hours.

I was there last night, thought Firebird. *Looking up at that building. I was in the city.*

It seemed like a dream now—the fountains, the plaza,

the fancy shop, the bird corpses—and the fascination and panic and fear she'd felt. Setting the bird free—that had been the best. Even better than seeing her purses on display. But what about the man with the hot breath in the subway? Firebird shuddered. Had that man really once owned Swamp Dog?

No wonder Swamp Dog ran away, thought Firebird.

The billboard was there, like always—you couldn't ignore it. It cast its looming shadow over their house and yard. But Firebird thought, *I'm not going billboard gazing today*. The Firebird that had done that—so dreamy, so gullible—seemed gone forever.

Then she heard noises. They came from the other side of the billboard—a revving engine, thumps, clattering. But Firebird didn't panic; she knew those sounds. No strangers were invading the swamp. It was just the guy who came to clean the billboard.

Firebird had watched him sometimes, hidden in the grass. He was a weary old guy who drove his truck through the scrubland, then climbed ladders to wash off the traffic grime with long-handled brushes. He'd been coming for years and years, ever since Trapper was a boy. He wasn't any threat to the Tuckers. If he knew about them, he didn't care. He just did his job and drove away.

Firebird paused in the yard, shocked by a sudden feeling of recklessness. She fought it, but didn't win. As she crawled under the billboard, she asked herself, *What the hell are you doing?*

This wasn't allowed. All her life she'd been warned against it. *Stay away from strangers*, that was the family rule.

But she'd already broken so many family rules. She was breaking them all the time—unlocking Gran's cupboard, talking to Dr. Pinker, going to the city in defiance of her dead mom's wishes. Keeping old Hog waiting for his breakfast.

Don't talk to strangers. The words echoed in her head. But if her own family wouldn't tell her the truth, who else could she talk to?

The old guy was up his ladder, so it was easy for Firebird, still clutching the blue plastic box, to wriggle a little way through the scrubland, then stand up, so it looked as if she'd just arrived from the other direction.

She had a sudden flashback to the man in the subway and almost ducked down again. But this man was up a ladder. He was old and slow. She could easily outrun him.

Act dumb, Firebird reminded herself. That was one family rule she didn't plan to break.

"Hi," she called up.

The billboard cleaner, looking down, saw a slight, fidgety girl with wild, ginger hair. He said, "Where'd you spring from?"

Firebird looked blank. So he said, "What's your name?"

Warning bells clanged in Firebird's head. If she told him, she was breaking the ultimate rule: *Never, ever tell anyone about the family.*

But she knew from talking to Dr. Pinker that if you wanted strangers to stay friendly, you'd better be friendly back. So, with her mind still shrieking out warnings, she told him, "Firebird." Straight after, she thought, *Why didn't you just lie?* But it was too late.

She wanted to ask the man about an ad. It had been on the billboard a long time ago. But Firebird could remember every poster she'd ever seen on the billboard—she took it for granted that he could, too. And if he couldn't, Firebird could remind him. From Gran's description, Firebird knew every detail of that particular ad. Down to the *V* shape the cigarettes made when they poked out of the packet.

Would it mean anything if the guy told her there'd never been any such ad? Yes, it would. In Firebird's mind it would be the proof she needed. Proof that Gran was lying about the day the angel came to the swamp. And that she'd just made up the ad to make it seem more real.

But nothing was happening the way Firebird planned it. The man stared down and said, "Firebird? I've never heard that name before. Where's that come from?"

And in her agitation, because she wasn't thinking straight and because she wanted to keep the stranger sweet, Firebird let slip some more private family information.

"I'm named Firebird after the Pontiac Firebird ad that was on the billboard the day I was born," Firebird told the man, like she was reciting a well-learned lesson.

She'd already decided not to ask him about the cigarette ad. She'd been crazy to talk to him at all. Hog's bell was ringing, calling her back to the swamp. She could hear it even here, beyond the billboard.

She was about to plunge back into the bushes, make her escape, when the man said, "I've been cleaning this billboard for thirty years. Most ads I don't remember. But I *know* there's never been one for a Pontiac Firebird. I can swear to that."

Firebird just stared at him. At first she didn't take in what he'd said.

"It was a big red car," she told him, "with tail fins."

"Nope," said the man, shaking his head firmly. "*No way* would I have forgotten that. When I was a youngster, a red Pontiac Firebird was my dream car. I was desperate to have one—course, I never could afford it."

He was coming back down the ladder, still talking. Firebird panicked and dropped to the ground like a hare. She lay flat among the bushes, her heart pounding. She heard the man shouting, "Hey! Where'd you get to?" But he wasn't curious enough to search around. He had another job to go to. He just shook his head, packed up his gear, and drove off.

When the sound of his truck engine had merged with the highway traffic, Firebird stood up. A 707 screamed over, like a silver knife ripping the sky open.

Firebird stood there a long time. Then she realized she was still clutching the blue box.

Got to feed Hog, she told herself.

She crawled back under the billboard and stumbled into the swamp.

11

Firebird plodded through the swamp, carrying Hog's breakfast in the blue plastic box.

Although she often daydreamed of distant places, Firebird's sense of belonging to the swamp had been strong—deeply rooted in the Tucker family history and the stories Gran told.

Those foundations of her life that had seemed rock solid were slipping away, one by one, right from under her feet. Now even her own name was in doubt. What the billboard cleaner had said, more than all the other lies she'd uncovered, threw her mind into chaos. She hardly knew who she was anymore.

That guy just forgot about the ad, Firebird tried to persuade herself.

Why should she believe some stupid old man?

But he'd seemed so sure. "There's never been one for a Pontiac Firebird," he'd said. "I can swear to that."

If she wasn't named after a car, then what was she named after? Was her real name even Firebird?

She tried to put a brake on her thoughts. It was driving her crazy, all this feverish speculation. There was only one way to settle it.

You've got to find out the truth, Firebird told herself. *Just ask Gran.*

That sounded like a simple solution. But Firebird was realizing that Gran was tricky, as slippery as an eel. She could get you to believe that black was white.

Yeah, Firebird mocked herself, *but you made it easy for her, didn't you? You said, "Oh, tell me that story again, Gran. Please, please. Tell me about the red shoes, the Pontiac Firebird, the day Dad brought Mom's angel to the swamp, and the big golden cigarette packet on the billboard."*

Bitterly, Firebird mimicked her own childish voice begging for more bedtime stories. "You were such a sucker," she jeered. So starry-eyed and unquestioning. Well, not anymore. Where there'd been stars in her eyes there was now only suspicion.

Firebird passed the angel, her stone hands pressed together, praying piously under the water, her cold, beautiful face staring up. And around her fingers was twined a withered garland. It was the daisy chain Ford had flung into the creek yesterday.

Suddenly, Firebird found herself wishing the angel could talk.

"You'd tell me the truth, wouldn't you?" said Firebird. You could trust an angel. Surely an angel wouldn't lie?

But maybe this one would. Maybe she was just a sham,

part of Gran's lies like the billboard ads, and not Mom's memorial at all.

Firebird felt desolate and entirely alone, as if there was no one in all the world left to turn to.

What about Ford? a voice whispered inside her head. Couldn't she confide in him? But she and her twin brother had never shared their problems. And Ford worshipped Trapper—he'd do whatever he said.

Maybe, thought Firebird, feeling more and more para-noid, *he's on* their *side. Conspiring with Gran and Trapper to keep her in the dark about all sorts of things . . .*

There was Hog's bell. It had been drowned out for a few minutes by a police helicopter buzzing overhead. Fire-bird hurried on.

He'll be in a mean mood when you get there, she thought. Hog didn't like to be kept waiting.

Hog was slithering out of his pool when Firebird ar-rived, heaving his heavy, white coils onto the grass.

"No," said Firebird. "I'm here. Get back in."

When Hog saw her, he let himself slide back into the pool so just his snout and his little red eyes were showing.

Firebird gave a deep, shaky sigh of relief. "Good Hog," she said.

"He wasn't really leaving the swamp," she reassured herself. He'd just gotten tired of waiting for his breakfast and had been going out to snatch a moorhen off the nest, or a rat.

And anyway, it was just another of Gran's stories, about their luck running out if Hog left. Firebird had to remind herself that she didn't believe those stories anymore.

"All right, all right," said Firebird nervously as Hog thrashed and snapped. "Breakfast's coming." She wasn't used to Hog. She'd almost never fed him; that was always Gran's job.

She ripped off the top of the plastic box. She had forgotten the toasting fork; she'd have to be careful, keep her fingers clear of his jaws.

Then Firebird saw what she'd pulled out, hidden among the kitchen scraps. It was the dead body of a tiny bird—the hummingbird from the plaza, with its red throat feathers missing.

So that's how Gran got rid of the birds after she'd plucked out their most colorful feathers. She fed them to Hog.

Shuddering, Firebird threw the bird's body away from her. She didn't dare look in the box again, just dumped it into Hog's pool. He grabbed something and swirled down into the depths.

Firebird slumped on her knees by the pool, fighting back nausea. All her city memories from last night came flooding back, overwhelming her. Then she heard the *phut-phut-phut* of an unfamiliar boat engine. She had enough presence of mind to hurl herself into the reeds.

She lay full length on the squelchy ground and made herself a little spy hole in the reeds. *Maybe it's Dr. Pinker,* she thought, *coming back to look for the angel, in another boat, not her canoe.* But when the boat came up the creek, Firebird could see straight away that it wasn't Dr. Pinker.

"It's the FWS people," she whispered, reading the letters on their life jackets. It looked like the two guys Dad had told them about. Alarmed, Firebird flattened herself right down in the reeds.

They're lucky Dad's home sick, she thought.

Dad would've challenged them, said, "What the hell do you think you're doing here?" She wondered where Ford was. He was just as uptight as Trapper about strangers invading the swamp. But maybe he'd already gone back to the house with the eel catch.

The strangers weren't cruising by. They'd stopped the engine and were climbing out onto the bank. Even well-hidden, Firebird felt a shiver of fear. She was thinking about the man in the subway.

They were talking. One, the bearded one, said as he moored the boat, "Wish I knew for sure who smashed that solar panel. I've got a pretty good idea, though."

The other one, the tall one, shrugged and said mildly, "You mean that eel trapper? He seemed friendly enough."

Beardface said, "I just didn't like the look in his eyes."

They peered into Hog's pool, but there was nothing to see. The sly old monster had sensed strangers. He was hidden away, deep down in the mud.

Then the tall one stooped, picked something up. "Hey, look at this."

Through her spy hole, Firebird saw what he had on his palm. It was the dead hummingbird she'd thrown away in disgust.

"Wonder why it fell here?" he said, examining the body. "It's usually that searchlight that gets them. Screws up their navigational systems." He squinted in the sun toward the tallest tower on the city skyline.

"You seen the plaza lately?" he asked Beardface. "It's like a massacre every night. Those birds are just flying over the city. But once they fall down between the skyscrapers they don't stand a chance. Too disoriented—they can't even *see* the sky to take off again."

"Someone should just smash that damn light," said Beardface. "It's a death trap for migrating birds. Do it myself if I thought I could get away with it."

The tall one put the bird's corpse gently back on the grass. They were going away. Firebird waited until she heard the outboard fade before she came out from her hiding place.

FORD wasn't back at the house like Firebird thought. He was proud of himself. He'd got a great catch of eels. They were thrashing about, making slime in plastic buckets on deck. Everything had gone really well; Dad would be pleased.

Ford had a sudden brain wave. He thought, *Why don't I save Dad a job? Go to the smokery for him?*

It irked him the way Dad and Gran had shouted no this morning when he'd suggested it, like they didn't think he could be trusted. It hurt his pride. *I'll show 'em*, thought Ford. He could do it, no problem.

The smokery would take live eels, too. The only reason Gran killed and skinned them first was for Firebird's stupid purses. *Well, she can do without her purses for once*, thought Ford. They weren't important. It was eel catching that paid the bills, bought them their new boat.

Dad was sick. *So I'm in charge*, thought Ford. It was up to him to make the decisions, to be the boss.

So Ford steered the boat along Flood Creek toward the river. He felt a sudden exhilaration. Going to the smokery and doing it alone, without Dad, felt like a big adventure.

There was a lot of water in Flood Creek today and it was rising. *Dad would probably say, "We'll stay in the swamp, son, not go out into open water."* Ford chuckled to himself. He idolized his father, but even he had to admit Trapper was sometimes way too cautious. Even if Hog's bell rang, just a little bit between meals, he'd say, "Bad weather on the way, Ford, best be careful."

But the sky was clear and blue over the swamp. There were some black clouds packed on the far horizon, but they were a long way off. The boat skimmed over the water.

When he steered her out from the sheltered swamp creeks into the river, Ford felt a sudden twinge of doubt. Vast stretches of open water faced him. He was alone in a very small boat in a very big world.

But then he felt the thrill of the surging river, the spray, the wide-open space after the swamp's confinement. The boat was flying along. No mosquitoes here; the wind whisked them away. And the air was fresh and breezy instead of hot and sticky.

Ford kept close to the bank, away from the big ships carving out swells in the river's main channel.

His face broke into a huge, excited grin, like a kid who wakes up on Christmas morning. Ford had to watch himself when he worked alongside Trapper, make sure he didn't do anything wrong, let Dad down. And now he was off the leash.

Drunk with freedom, Ford let out a wild rebel whoop.

He scared off a cormorant, standing on a rock like a crucifix, drying out its wings.

Careful, though, Ford warned himself, struggling to make his face solemn again. This was a serious mission, not some joyride. He had to act grown-up, responsible. Dad was sick at home, depending on him. But Ford grinned again; he just couldn't help himself.

Can't wait to see Dad's face, he thought, *when I walk in with a fistful of cash from the smokery.*

12

Before, Firebird thought that the city had no connection with the Tuckers' lives. But now she knew different.

You always thought Ford was the dumb one, Firebird reproached herself. But she'd been dumber. For years Gran had been feeding her all sorts of downright lies, sketchy stories, and she'd swallowed them whole, taken them all as gospel.

An hour had passed since she'd overheard the FWS guys talking. She hadn't gone back home, not even to see if Dad was any better. She'd spent the time wandering around aimlessly in the swamp. And her eyes were drawn again and again to the glittering towers of the city, where Gran made secret trips to sell her purses and collect the shattered bodies of birds to decorate them.

Firebird had been so proud, seeing her purses in that shop. But she wasn't going to make any more, no way, not now that she knew where the feathers came from.

But that seemed like a feeble protest. That wouldn't stop the nightly massacre, would it? Firebird felt sick when she thought about it—those beautiful migrating birds, lured to their deaths by the searchlight on top of the tallest tower.

But what could she do about it? She felt helpless again, all tangled up in a world she couldn't control.

Suddenly, Beardface's words slammed into her head: *"Someone should just smash that damn light."*

That's what I'll do! thought Firebird wildly.

It was a mad idea—impossible! But she didn't even stop to think about it. "I'm going to smash that thing good!" she muttered.

All fired up, she started racing toward the billboard and almost tripped over Ford. He'd moored the boat in Judith's Creek and was sitting on the bank, just sitting, staring into space.

Firebird wasn't even going to stop; she had something really important to do. But Ford turned dull eyes toward her. "Dad lied to me," he said.

"What?" said Firebird impatiently. She wasn't even looking at him. Her eyes were fixed on the horizon, on the city's proudest, tallest tower. Somewhere on its roof was the killer searchlight.

I'm going to smash that damn thing into little pieces, thought Firebird. *And stomp on the pieces.*

That one purpose had fixed itself into her head. Like it was the best, the biggest protest she could make. And it wasn't just about the birds. It was about all the other stuff, too. The way she'd been lied to by people she loved and respected.

"The smokery's closed," Ford was telling her. "Gone bust. I've just been there, seen it all boarded up. And this guy fishing told me, 'There's no money in eels anymore. The bottom fell clean out of the business. Thought everyone knew that.' And he looked at me like I was some kind of idiot."

He waited for Firebird's horrified reaction. But she didn't seem surprised, as if it wasn't even news. And why was she staring at the city skyline like that? What could she see that he couldn't?

At last, Firebird dragged her eyes away and looked at her brother. "I told you they lied," was all she said. "They're lying about all sorts of things. Telling us great big fat lies all the time. Like we're idiots."

She was shifting from foot to foot, desperate to be gone. But Ford felt lonelier than he'd ever felt before. For once in his life he needed his twin sister's company. He needed someone he could trust.

But Firebird had already turned away. Her eyes were fixed on that tallest tower, as if searing its shape into her brain. Then she said, "See that tower? That's where I'm going. Right to the top."

"But that's in the city!" said Ford, appalled, as if Firebird intended a trip into hell. "We don't go to the city. Dad hates the city."

He didn't say, "Mom hated it, too." Because for some reason, Trapper never used that kind of emotional blackmail on Ford. As if it was only Firebird who should be bound by Mom's wishes and needed to be constantly reminded.

"I've already been once," said Firebird, her voice defiant and proud. "I followed Gran last night."

"Gran went to the city?" said Ford. "I don't believe you."

"Oh, wake up!" said Firebird. "You already found out that Dad lied, didn't you?"

"How'd you get there?" demanded Ford.

"You go under the billboard," Firebird told him, as if she was rehearsing the way in her head. "Down through the scrubland. Then under the overpass. Then you walk through the storm drains, then through the tunnels . . ."

She stopped after she'd said *tunnels*, chilled by sudden fear. But she shook it off. Nothing, not even that scary guy, was going to stop her now.

For the first time in twenty-four hours she felt she had control over her life. That she was calling the shots.

"Swamp Dog knows the way," said Firebird.

But she couldn't wait for Swamp Dog. She had to smash that light before nightfall, stop the next massacre.

Then she was off and running.

"Don't go to the city," Ford called after her. "Stay here." He sounded afraid, as if he was scared of being left alone. As if he was scared she might never come back.

He was relieved when Firebird flung over her shoulder, "Don't worry. I won't be long."

Then suddenly, she skidded to a stop and spun around as if she'd just thought of something. Ford had never seen his sister like this. Her eyes, usually so dreamy, blazed with a fierce and cunning intensity. "And don't tell *them* I've gone. Right? Whatever you do, don't tell them *anything.*"

"But what are you going to the city *for?*" asked Ford.

For a split second, he almost said, "I'll come with you," because Firebird shouldn't go to such a dangerous place on her own. But going to the city was such a big family taboo; it went against everything that Dad had taught him. And Ford was still trying desperately to be loyal to him. To cling to the old beliefs even though they were crumbling into dust all around him.

And anyway, it was too late to make the offer. The reeds had already swallowed Firebird up, leaving Ford staring after her like an abandoned child.

Firebird had to pass by the house to get to the billboard. She didn't plan to stop. She saw Trapper puttering weakly around the yard; he looked a bit better. Then she changed her mind and did stop. She needed to take something with her to smash the searchlight. She found a grappling hook on the landing stage.

She did one other thing. She crept around the back of the house and climbed in her bedroom window. She made a hump under her duvet with two pillows. If Gran looked in, she'd think Firebird was in bed.

"Just doing like you said, Gran, being a good little girl, sleeping off my bad mood," muttered Firebird as she patted the pillows into a convincing body shape.

The thought of deceiving Gran, that archdeceiver, gave Firebird a thrill of satisfaction.

Then she climbed back out of the window and was off again, swinging the grappling hook by her side. But her shoulders prickled as if she expected Gran to yell after her any second, "Hey, you get back here!"

She wriggled under the billboard. She didn't look up at its message. It was just another delusion.

She bit her lip to stop it from trembling and set off through the scrubland.

The last time Firebird had come this far beyond the billboard it had been night. In the harsh glare of day, everything looked different. She couldn't hide in the shadows. And she could see people, or at least their blurred faces, inside cars as the highway traffic roared by.

Were they staring at her? A wild-haired girl, swinging a grappling hook like a weapon? Firebird didn't care. She was too focused on what she had to do.

She ducked into the gloom under the overpass pillars. The deafening roar became a rumbling echo. The earth shook, not just now and then like last night, but constantly, from subway trains. It felt hot, too, as if there was a volcano down there. Steam came up through grills in the ground.

At first Firebird couldn't find the right storm drain. Now that it was daylight, she saw that there were several of them, fanning out in different directions. But which one led to the city?

Why didn't you bring Swamp Dog? she fumed at herself. *You're already lost.*

Then she saw the dead tree wedged in one concrete trench—the tree she'd climbed to get out of the storm drains.

Firebird's troubled face broke into a grin. She wasn't lost—she'd found the way.

Firebird made it safely through the drains. But in the subway, she held the grappling hook so tightly that her knuckles were bone white. Her eyes flickered everywhere. Once, a rat scuttling out of a side passage made her shriek out loud. But she didn't see that man again. As she got close to the city center, a few pedestrians joined her from other white-tiled tunnels. Firebird's heart fluttered madly. But they walked briskly, staring ahead. They didn't come close, or even look at her.

At last, there were the steps that led out of the tunnels. Firebird started climbing them. It was just past noon when she emerged into the sunshine of the plaza.

BACK in the swamp, Ford was still sitting, just as Firebird had left him. It seemed like he'd sit like that forever. He hadn't even *begun* to think yet, to try to sort things out in his head. All he knew was that his future, which before had stretched so clear ahead of him, had suddenly dissolved into smoke and shadows.

But that was nothing compared to the hurt and bewilderment he felt now that he'd found out Dad had been lying to him. When he'd thought Trapper was treating him like an adult, trusting him.

From the densest part of the swamp, Hog's bell was ringing, even though he'd had his breakfast. Ford didn't hear it. The day was darkening; the storm clouds were on the move, coming closer. Ford didn't notice. At last, he moved. But it was only to crawl back down the bank to the boat. The eels were still there, squirming around in their buckets. Ford lifted the buckets, and one by one, dumped the eels over the side and watched them wriggle back down into the mud.

Ford got a tarpaulin out of the boat locker. He spread it out on the deck boards. Then he crept under it and lay curled up, with his whole body, even his head, completely hidden.

13

THE plaza wasn't eerily empty like it had been last night. It was alive with busy people rushing in all directions. From the café tables where Gran had stopped to smoke came the burble of voices and the chink of coffee cups.

Firebird shrank back, alarmed at first by the noise and bustle and hid the grappling hook under her jacket. But no one was looking at her. She might as well have been invisible.

The tallest tower was on the other side of the plaza. Somewhere on its roof was the searchlight she'd come to destroy.

Firebird joined the crowd and crossed the plaza. City pigeons pecked around her feet like chickens. The searchlight didn't bother them. When it was switched on, they were in their roosts, fast asleep. Only the migrating birds that flew over at night, navigating by the stars, fell victim to it.

At the tallest tower's entrance, Firebird was caught up in a surge of people. She was hustled in with them through the glass rotating door and was spewed out on the other side.

Now she was in the lobby with carpet under her feet, a reception desk and security guards nearby, but still she couldn't stop. As people streamed toward the elevators she was caught in the crowd. Firebird had never been in an elevator before. She was crammed close to a man's armpit, getting whiffs of his sweat and spicy deodorant, as machinery whirred and the elevator rose. Under her jacket, the grappling hook dug into her ribs.

The elevator whisked her upward. People pushed past her to get out, then others got in. Firebird felt helpless again in these alien surroundings. She didn't know what to do, how things worked. Everything was happening far too fast. She didn't have time to think.

And then she was alone in the elevator with one young woman. The woman stared into space, humming to herself.

The doors opened again. The woman clicked out in her high heels. Firebird thought she would just walk away. But the woman turned around, made eye contact, then spoke. "Excuse me," she said. "But where is your security pass?"

At last, Firebird's brain reacted. She shot out of the elevator like a startled rabbit. "Hey!" the young woman called after her.

But Firebird had already raced around a corner. Keeping out of sight came naturally to Firebird; she'd had years of practice in the swamp. And it helped that the offices were nearly all empty; most people were out to lunch.

Firebird roamed the corridors. She didn't have a clue what went on in this building, what people did here. She was only looking for one thing—the steps to the roof. She found them behind a door marked FIRE EXIT. When she was climbing them, a tiny, scared voice in her head wailed, *What are you* doing *here? Have you gone completely mad?*

Another fire door opened onto the roof. When she went through it, Firebird's heart was hammering, sweat prickling under her arms. But suddenly, her resolve came powering back, ten times as strong. She *must* smash that searchlight. Not only to save the birds, but crazily, to save herself, too.

"It's *here*," she whispered, as if somehow she'd expected it not to be.

Rising above water tanks, antennae, satellite dishes, and all the other junk on the roof was the searchlight, mounted on top of a pyramid of latticed ironwork.

It wasn't what Firebird had expected. She'd assumed it was just one big, rotating light. But it wasn't that simple. It was a circle of six lights that were switched on in sequence—that meant a lot more glass to smash.

She was trampling on bird corpses, some fresh, some long dead, as she crossed the roof. They hadn't tumbled down between the skyscrapers. They'd flown along the beams and crashed straight into the lights.

It was a grisly, scrunching carpet. But Firebird smiled as she gripped the grappling hook. She wasn't confused anymore. She knew exactly what she had to do.

Even the spectacular view didn't distract her. Out on the river, there was a sinister, gray veil, slanting between sky and water. It was the kind of violent, torrential cloudburst that was becoming more common in this part of the world.

But Firebird didn't see the bad weather sneaking up. She was standing at the base of the iron pyramid, squinting up into the sun, gusty wind whipping her hair. She was going to have to do some climbing.

But suddenly, through the sun haze, she saw golden eyes staring down at her, and cruel, hooked beaks.

There are birds up there!

It was a pair of city hawks, who used the searchlights as a daytime perch.

Firebird didn't know it, but hawks thrived up there, mostly due to the searchlight, which gave them a plentiful food supply: Birds dazed by its beam were easy prey.

Firebird started climbing. She kept an eye on the hawks. They ruffled their feathers but didn't do anything. Just watched her every move. When she got halfway up the pyramid, they suddenly swooped away.

Good, thought Firebird. That fierce, unflinching, golden gaze had unnerved her.

Clinging on with one hand and taking a wild, swinging blow, Firebird smashed the first light. It fell in glittering shards all over her, then showered down among the bird corpses. She worked her way around, smashing the others. She put her heart and soul into it, attacking those lights with furious violence—savage, screaming cries of rage. And it felt great. Like a wonderful, joyful release.

She'd reached the last light when the hawks attacked her.

They came diving back in, from opposite directions, screeching. They buffeted her head with sharp wing blows.

Then they went for her face, slashing at flesh, trying to claw her eyes. But Firebird hadn't finished what she came to do. Blindly, she struck out at the last light. Glass showered into her hair.

The female hawk dived in, talons out, and ripped her earlobe. Firebird yelled, dropped the grappling hook and half slid, half fell, back down the pyramid. Whirling her arms around her head, she ran for the fire door.

But they followed her, screeching with rage at the threatening stranger who'd invaded their territory. They dived again and again, trying to drive her away. They didn't know that she meant no harm to their two chicks in a nest on a top-floor window ledge.

Firebird threw herself behind the door. She could hear their shrill, savage shrieks, hear them raking at the steel with their talons, trying to get at her.

She crouched on the staircase, gasping, shuddering. There was something wet trickling down her face. She wiped it and thought, in a surprised way, *It's blood.* There seemed to be an awful lot of it. She licked it off her fingers and tasted salt. After a while, the hawks' cries stopped. They'd given up and gone back to their chicks.

Firebird smeared her face again with her sleeve and tried to stop shaking. She had to get out of there. Maybe that woman had already alerted security.

She scurried back through the second fire door, into the carpeted corridor. This time people did stare at her, looking shocked, and tried to question her. But Firebird acted like they didn't exist. She walked right by them, her back stiff, her eyes staring straight ahead, her face bloody. She took the elevator down, alone. In it, she tried to clean herself up.

I'm bleeding all over the place, she thought. And suddenly, her legs felt weak and wobbly, as if she was going to collapse.

Then the elevator stopped at the ground floor and the doors opened. Firebird staggered out, hurried through the lobby before the guards could stop her. She heard them shouting behind her.

Only when she was well clear of the building, and swallowed up in the city crowds, did she feel safe again.

14

FORD didn't know how long he'd been lying curled up under the tarpaulin. It was almost as if he'd put himself into suspended animation. He wasn't moving or thinking. He wasn't aware of his surroundings.

But even Ford was finding it hard to pretend that nothing had happened, that everything was the same as before.

Every so often, rogue thoughts would flicker like tiny flames. *Dad lied. There's no smokery. There's no future.* And: *Where's he getting the money?*

But Ford snuffed out those thoughts before they could become raging infernos and sank back into his state of frozen misery.

But then, at last, something did make Ford react. He only gradually became aware of it—a pattering on the tarpaulin, like drumbeats; a hissing on the water all around the boat.

Raindrops? wondered Ford indifferently.

Then he heard something else. Out in the swamp, Hog's bell was ringing—shrill, insistent.

What's that old devil want? thought Ford, not much caring.

But slowly, like a frog coming out of hibernation, his other senses were waking up; he couldn't stop them. Now he could feel the boat rocking, lifting as if on a sudden surge of water.

Whoa, thought Ford, rolling around in the bottom. *What's going on?*

Slosh—cold creek water came into the boat, a big wave of it. It hit the tarpaulin, gushed underneath, and drenched him.

Move! Ford ordered himself. *What are you lying around here for?*

Then he felt the boat straining, shaking. The creek was trying to carry it away. Ford knew his mooring, a rope tied to a willow, wouldn't hold.

Fully alert now, he thought, *Judith's Creek is flooding!*

That had never happened before. If even Judith's Creek was flooding, what was Flood Creek, the swamp's main channel, doing?

Ford scrambled out from under the tarpaulin into a different world: dark, wild, filled with rain and swirling water. The boat was bucking madly. He hurled himself at the bank and nearly didn't make it. The flood tried to suck him back in. Grasping slippery grass with both hands, Ford hauled himself out of reach of the creek. Judith's Creek was spilling over its banks, running faster than he'd ever seen it.

Frantically, he tried to retie the mooring rope. Too late. It was torn out of his hands and their new, expensive boat was whisked away, bobbing lightly as an eggshell on the flood.

Ford couldn't believe it. He stared after the boat.

"What's Dad gonna say?" he moaned. "Dad will go ballistic." That was their livelihood down the drain, their eel-fishing business ruined. But then Ford remembered that their business didn't exist anyway. That it was just a big sham.

But he had no time to brood about that. He had to get back to the house before he was cut off. The house, raised on stilts, should be safe.

He ran. The geography of the swamp was second nature to him; he instinctively chose the driest paths, the highest ground. But the swamp was like a great soggy sponge, water spurting up everywhere. He was splashing in it; even the willow islands weren't safe.

The rain was stopping. There were just big, fat drops now. The clouds were scattering, the sun was shining again in a blue sky. But that was deceptive. Because the damage had already been done—by that sudden, ferocious storm dumping millions of gallons of rain into an already swollen river. The river couldn't cope. It had burst its banks and that was causing a flash flood in the swamp.

The river had overflowed before, but never like this, so fast or so violently. Flood Creek was raging, boiling, throwing spray seventy feet into the sky. It was carrying debris—whole willow trees torn up by their roots—along with it.

Ford was almost at the house. He could see it was safe, the flood swirling around the stilts it was raised on. But the storm surge wasn't stopping there. As Ford waded knee-deep through the yard, among the floating eel traps, he saw a second tidal wave, a foamy brown torrent, creeping toward the billboard.

Ford stopped and stared. That had never happened. After a bad storm, the swamp had always been able to swallow the excess water. It had sometimes got as far as the house. But that was only a couple of times. It had never, ever gone beyond the billboard.

And then another thought struck Ford like a punch in the belly: *Firebird's gone to the city.* He struggled to remember what she'd told him; he'd hardly been paying attention. She'd said, *"Don't worry. I won't be long."* But hadn't she said something about walking through storm drains? Ford didn't know much about the city, but he knew what storm drains were for. When the flood reached the city's outskirts, they would break up its force, divert it back to the river or deep underground, so the city would be safe. What if Firebird was coming back down those drains? Now, this minute? She'd meet the flood head-on.

"Maybe she's already back home," Ford tried to reassure himself. "I bet she is. I bet she's safe back home."

At the top of the steps the kitchen door was flung open. It was Trapper, a shivering wreck, sick again, his eyes red-rimmed and hollow.

"Thank god you're safe," he said to Ford. "What are you standing out there for? That flood's still rising."

And now Gran was behind Trapper. Ford had never

seen her in such a state. She looked helpless, distraught. Her voice was near hysterical. "Firebird's not in her bedroom. I looked in before. I thought she was asleep but she's gone—"

"I know where she is," Ford interrupted her. "I'll go get her."

"Tell me where she is," said Trapper. "I'll go."

But halfway down the steps his knees sagged. He had to hang on to the rail to stop himself from falling. "Damn," he muttered, raging at his own weakness, "damn, damn." But he still ordered Ford, "Get inside."

And Gran was saying something like, "Listen to your dad . . ."

Ford stood, indecisive. He didn't know what to do—he was so used to following his father's orders. The flood swirled, eel traps knocked against his knees, eel skins fluttered on the line above his head.

"Get inside," said Trapper again.

Trapper put a hand to his head, swaying as if he were going to pass out. Ford splashed forward. "You all right, Dad?"

Trapper waved him away. "You going to do as you're told and get in here?"

Ford swallowed nervously, but there was no help for it. He saw that he was going to have to defy his father and take matters into his own hands.

"Look, Dad," said Ford, "you can't hardly stand up. How are you going to go and get Firebird?"

"I'm all right, I'm all right," insisted Trapper, forcing himself to stand upright on shaky legs.

But by then Ford was already sploshing out of the yard. "Just tell us where she is!" Gran shouted after him.

But Ford remembered what Firebird had said: "Don't tell them *anything*."

"I'll bring her back!" he yelled over his shoulder. "Don't worry. You stay there."

Then he crammed his hands over his ears so he couldn't hear their voices anymore.

There was already water flowing under the billboard when Ford reached it, twisting its way through the weeds and long grass. Before he wriggled under himself, he glanced behind him. The swamp was roaring now, churning with water, with the river pumping in more every minute. And the storm surge, ten feet deep and rising, was heading that way, carrying eel traps, fuel drums, and tree branches along with it.

Ford didn't stop to watch. He dived under the billboard and hauled himself out the other side, dripping wet.

He was beyond the billboard—somewhere he'd never been before, not even to look at the ads. It should have been a big deal for him, but it made hardly any impact at all on his mind. All he cared about was getting to Firebird before the floodwater did.

He stopped, confused by the unfamiliar landscape, unsure which way to go. He wished Dad was with him. But Dad was too sick to help.

Swamp Dog knows the way, thought Ford, suddenly remembering what Firebird had said. But that was no use to him now. Swamp Dog was probably drowned.

Cars and trucks streamed by on the highway, rainbows dancing all around them in the spray hissing up from the wet road. But the storm surge wasn't going to go that way. The water that had already snaked under the billboard was following the slope of the land, flowing away from the highway, through the scrubland, and disappearing between the gray concrete pillars of the overpass.

Ford set off to follow it, hoping it would lead to the storm drains. If Firebird was coming back through them, she'd have no idea what danger she was in. The day was so deceptively calm and sunny again. Who could guess what nature was about to unleash?

Ford knew the storm surge was coming. But even he was shocked by the booming explosion behind him as it slammed into the billboard.

He knew he should run. But he couldn't help turning around. "Jesus!"

The water seemed to be swallowing the billboard up, bursting around it, even over the top.

One second, the billboard, with its bright, enticing pictures, promised "LIVE YOUR DREAMS!" The next it was gone, lost behind a muddy waterfall.

Ford started running then. The water was already carving a fast-moving stream through the scrubland. In minutes, that would be a tidal wave.

Behind him, the mighty fortress wall of the billboard, its foundations weakened by the greater power of the storm surge, started to rock.

15

FIREBIRD was almost through the storm drains. A few minutes more and she'd be out of them. Then through the scrubland, under the billboard, and home.

She carried the knowledge of what she'd just done like a jewel shining in her mind. *I did it. I smashed the searchlight. I smashed it all to pieces!*

But then something else took her attention. She wondered why she was suddenly splashing through water. The scummy puddles had become a fast-flowing trickle. Firebird shrugged. It was hardly enough to wet her shoes. And she'd be out of this storm drain any second. She could see the dead tree ahead, ghostly white in the gloom.

Firebird was climbing its branches when she heard a low, growling sound.

What's that? She thought it was just heavy traffic overhead.

Then it swelled to a rumbling roar, echoing like thunder under the overpass pillars, as if it were getting closer and closer. Firebird peered along the drain, still not understanding. One second there was nothing, the next a crashing wall of water came hurtling toward her.

Her mind barely had time to register terror before it hit her.

She was slammed against the branches. The water rushed onward, trying to drag her with it, but somehow she held on. It foamed over her head, into her eyes, nose, and mouth.

Firebird thought, *I'm drowning.*

Ford, under the overpass pillars, was calling her name. But his voice was lost in the roaring confusion.

Firebird felt the pull of the flood as it surged past her, battering her, trying to snatch her out of the tree. She clung monkeylike to a branch, wrapping her arms and legs around it. Her frantic brain was shrieking at her, *Don't let go! Don't let go!*

She managed to force her head above water. Choking, spluttering, she gasped in some air. But holding on took all her strength. Her hands were slipping and her arms were being wrenched out of their sockets. Then the tree she was hugging began to shudder. She gave a scream so shrill and despairing that Ford heard its echoes.

Ford yelled again, looked wildly around. All the storm drains were filled with tumbling water, racing along under huge pressure. The noise was deafening. "Where are you?" Firebird's shrieks came again. This time he looked in the right direction.

He saw white tree branches shaking and Firebird's hair streaming out like red seaweed strands.

"Firebird!"

Firebird saw him as he kneeled at the top of the drain, looking down at her. She was struggling to keep her head above water. Ford could hear the tree cracking and splintering. A branch snapped clean off and was whisked away in the flood.

"I can reach you," said Ford.

Ford threw himself down, full length, stretching out an arm. His fingertips were in the swirling water, but he couldn't quite reach Firebird.

"Come on, grab my hand."

"I can't!" screamed Firebird. She didn't dare let go of the tree.

But the flood was working the tree loose like a rotten tooth. And Firebird would be carried with it, into the darkness, toward the huge pipes that took the excess water underground. She felt the tree shudder again and start to move.

"Let go," Ford begged, his voice panicky. "You've got to. You'll get swept away."

Firebird was still screaming, "I can't!" as she reached out, grabbing one of Ford's wrists. He hauled her over to the side of the drain, pulling her clear of the water. Behind her the tree, with a terrible cracking sound, gave way and was swirled off in the flood.

Up on the sunlit Central Plaza, in the pavement café, people chatted and drank cappuccinos, unaware of the drama going on beneath them. The city's flood defenses were struggling to cope with the storm surge. Some of the underground pipes almost burst under the strain. But the defenses had held, just.

A hot splash of sunlight had found its way under the highway pillars. Firebird and Ford sat huddled in it. Firebird was too wrung out and shattered to move. Ford was sitting, head down, hands dangling between his knees. Finally, he raised his head and asked Firebird, "What happened to your face?"

Firebird stirred herself, as if waking from a dream. "Is it a mess?" she said, touching her face, sounding surprised. "Ow!" She'd found the ear the hawk had torn. She'd forgotten about that.

"We'd better go back," said Ford. "Gran and Dad'll be worrying."

Firebird showed no signs of shifting. She was soaking wet, bedraggled, and bleeding. Her clothes were steaming in the sunlight. She peeled off her jacket and squeezed some water out of her T-shirt. Then she gave up, shrugging hopelessly. "Look at me, I'm a mess," she said.

She saw Ford was studying her with an anxious, puzzled look, as if he was trying to understand but couldn't.

"What'd you want to go to the city for, anyway?" he burst out. "Us Tuckers don't go there. The city's got nothing we need."

Firebird didn't answer. But she started to cry, great shuddering sobs, her shoulders shaking. Ford looked on in distress. He didn't know what to do. He reached out his hand clumsily but then quickly drew it back. He'd learned lots of things from Trapper, but not how to deal with situations like this.

Now Firebird was saying something, between gulping sobs.

"What?" said Ford. "What?" It sounded like something about a searchlight. He couldn't make any sense of that.

Firebird lifted her face, where tears mixed with blood and river mud. She'd just smashed the searchlight, done something really great. So why was she suddenly falling to pieces, feeling so helpless and vulnerable? As if the slightest touch would bruise her?

She fought to get a grip on herself and give Ford some information that he'd understand.

"They've been selling my purses in the city," said Firebird. "In a really fancy shop."

"Come on," said Ford. "You're kidding me. Who'd want to buy your purses?"

"Think I'm lying to you, too?" Firebird burst out furiously. "I'm not like *them*." She dragged her hand over her face and smeared away the tears.

"I've seen my purses in that shop," she said, her voice calmer now. "With my own eyes. For sale for lots of money."

Ford was silent. He wanted to say, "You're kidding me," again. But he feared her anger.

When he didn't speak, Firebird thought he still hadn't got the point.

"That's where all the money must be coming from," said Firebird, "that Dad waves around, that he used to buy the boat. I mean, it isn't coming from eel trapping, is it?"

"I don't want to hear," Ford interrupted.

"But how does the shop get the money to them?" Firebird was wondering. "Because it's closed at night when

Gran goes. Maybe it's sent to the bank at Hook Bay, or the post office . . ."

Ford jammed his hands over his ears. "Shut up!"

He knew what Firebird said made sense. You didn't have to be a genius to work it all out. But he still had to deny it—it was just too devastating. It was tearing his world apart. He coped with it the only way he knew how, by lashing out at Firebird.

He took his hands off his ears and waved them around. He thrust his face aggressively into hers. "That's the biggest load of *crap* I've ever heard."

"Ask them," said Firebird. Her voice sounded world-weary, as if she just couldn't be bothered to argue anymore. "Just ask them where the money's coming from."

"Okay, I will!" Ford leaped up. "I'm going back to the house to ask them right now."

Firebird warned him, "Watch out. They'll probably just lie to you some more."

But she also knew a confrontation was long overdue. So she jumped up, too, to follow him. Then realized there was something else she'd meant to ask. "You didn't tell them where I'd gone, did you?"

"No," said Ford. "I didn't."

"Thanks," said Firebird, surprised. She'd half expected Ford to run straight to Dad, telling tales. "And thanks for coming to look for me. I wouldn't have gotten out of that drain if you hadn't . . ." She stopped awkwardly. She really wanted Ford to be on her side. But she could see that he didn't want to believe it, about the purses.

"That's crap," he was still muttering angrily. "I'm going to ask Dad."

He went stomping out from under the overpass with Firebird behind him. She felt sick with apprehension at the thought of the showdown to come. How would Gran and Dad react to Ford's questions? What would they say?

The sun's glare hammered into their faces, blinding them for a second.

Ford screwed up his eyes, then stared around him. He'd expected a lot more water. But there was only a trickle coming down through the scrubland. The flash flood was over, soon as it had begun. It had left devastation behind it, though. It looked like a line of tanks had been this way, battering down bushes and churning up the scrubland into a muddy battlefield.

Firebird was gazing to the west, at the tallest tower on the city skyline. She was thinking, *Was I really* up there? *Did I really smash that light?*

It seemed for a second as if it was just another delusion. Part of the lies that seemed to make up her life. But then she touched her ear, torn by the hawks, winced and knew that it was true.

Ford raised his eyes beyond the scrubland, toward the swamp and home. For a moment he felt giddy, his mind thrown totally off balance. What was going on? His gaze wasn't stopped by the billboard ad. It went straight through. He could see the swamp, even their house, as if the billboard had turned to glass.

Then he understood. There was no billboard anymore. It lay flat on the ground, smashed down by the storm surge.

Firebird felt Ford clutch her arm and heard him whisper, "Look," in a voice filled with awe and disbelief.

She turned around. And it took her minutes of shocked, dizzy staring to work it out, too. Where the billboard had been there was just a huge, gaping hole.

The Tuckers' private lives were suddenly a peep show. Every commuter on the highway would be able to see them going about their business. With a high-powered telescope, people in the city could probably zoom in on their backyard. See Gran bashing out eels' brains, then skinning them. Hanging the skins on the line to dry like washing.

Ford and Firebird gazed at each other, speechless.

Then Firebird said, as if she was still denying the evidence of her own eyes, "How could that have happened?"

She'd looked at the billboard almost every day. Ford had forgotten about it most of the time. But both of them had taken it for granted that it would shield them forever.

Ford said, "Dad will have a fit."

Even as he said it, he knew it was a serious understatement. Trapper had always hated strangers invading his territory, nosing around. But he'd got much worse lately. One webcam had driven him into a frenzy of destruction. Ford shook his head. Now a thousand eyes could spy on them. Even he couldn't predict what Dad might do.

"Maybe they'll put it back up by tomorrow," he said, as though, if that happened, their lives could go on just the same as before.

Above the traffic's roar, Firebird became aware of a wailing siren. At first she didn't take much notice. You could hear sirens from the city at all hours of the day and night.

But this siren didn't fade away into the city streets. Its squealing got louder and more frantic, as if it was heading their way. Firebird turned around. She saw a blue light flashing and a big, white, four-wheel drive bouncing through the scrubland toward them, with two men in the front.

Instinctively, she and Ford dropped to the ground, making themselves invisible in the undergrowth. "I think they saw us," said Ford, gripping her arm. "I swear they did."

If they did, they didn't stop. The vehicle plowed past them, lights flashing, sirens wailing. On the side, Firebird read: AMBULANCE.

The billboard was facedown, buried in mud and storm debris. Even so, Firebird expected the driver to stop at it, as if the barrier between the swamp and the city still existed. As if the billboard still had the power to keep out invaders. But the ambulance didn't stop. It drove right over the billboard and into the Tuckers' yard, where the flood had left eel traps, fuel drums, and splintered fish boxes heaped in a jumbled mess. It parked outside the Tuckers' back door. The two men leaped out and ran up the steps into the house.

"It's for Dad," said Firebird. "They've come to take Dad away."

"Don't be stupid," said Ford. "He'll get better. He doesn't need an ambulance."

It was unthinkable. Trapper's toughness and his self-reliance were legendary.

"Even when that winch wire cut him," Ford reminded Firebird, "he wouldn't go to the hospital."

But Firebird didn't hear him. She was already running toward the house.

16

"FIREBIRD!" said Gran. "Thank god you're safe."

The ambulance stood on soggy ground in the yard, its siren silent, but the blue light still flashing. Its back doors were flung wide open. The two paramedics were carrying Dad down the steps from the kitchen in some kind of chair thing, his head lolling back, an oxygen mask strapped to his face.

"Trapper's never going to forgive me," said Gran, twisting her hands in distress.

When the floodwaters had gone down, she'd run into the swamp looking for help. She'd had to go right down to the river. "There was a guy down there in a boat," she told Firebird. "He'd taken shelter from the storm. He had a phone. He called the ambulance for me."

"It wasn't one of those FWS guys, was it?" roared Ford, who'd just skidded into the yard. "What did you ask *him* for help for? Now he knows where we live."

Ford seemed to have forgotten that with the billboard

gone, every passing commuter would know where the Tuckers lived. There was no way to hide from prying eyes.

A red-haired woman had already made her taxi stop on the overpass, and was staring down at Trapper being carried out of the house.

"What's wrong with Dad?" Ford begged Gran as the paramedics manhandled Trapper into the ambulance.

"I don't know," Gran answered, rubbing her big, freckled arms in distress. "I just don't know. But he was burning up, then shivering, then he started raving, sounding like he was out of his mind. Then he just passed out and I shook him and shook him. I got really scared. I thought he was dead . . ."

"Dead?" Ford echoed the word, horrified.

"He'll be all right," said Gran hastily. "The doctors'll make him better."

Ford wasn't reassured. "What're they doing to him? Where're they taking him?"

"To a hospital," said Gran. "In the city." Ford's face seemed to crumple in despair. "I had to do *something*," protested Gran.

It was clear now that Trapper wasn't dead. The oxygen had brought him back around. And he wasn't going to go quietly. He was lashing out at the paramedics, shouting and cursing.

"Calm down," one of them said as they strapped him to the stretcher so he couldn't fight. "There's nothing to be scared of."

"You coming, Mrs. Tucker?" one of them asked Gran.

Gran climbed in. It looked for a minute like she was going to let Ford and Firebird come, too.

"Loreal," Trapper was raving. "You worthless bitch!"

"What did he say?" asked Firebird.

Gran glanced at her sharply. "Don't take no notice. He's out of his head, he doesn't know what he's saying." And suddenly she seemed to get a grip on herself and take charge again. "You two stay here," she ordered Ford and Firebird.

"But, Gran!" Ford was already climbing into the ambulance. "I want to go with Dad."

"No." Gran pushed Ford so hard out of the ambulance that he fell sprawling into the mud. "Do as you're told," she snapped. "Wait here. I'll be back soon."

Trapper was shouting out again, cursing someone, but they couldn't hear who.

One of the paramedics was in the cab, on the radio. He turned around to his partner. "We'll take him to the city hospital," he said. "That's closest."

Then he started the engine. The back doors closed. The spinning wheels sent up sprays of mud. For a minute it looked like the ambulance might get stuck. But it revved hard and went rocketing out of the yard and over the billboard, through that great gaping hole that let in the outside world.

Ford stared after it. In the scrubland it switched on its siren. They could see its windshield glinting in the sun and the blue light whirling. But then it disappeared into a dip. And after that, they didn't see it again; it was lost in the roaring traffic. They could still hear the siren, though—a thin, screeching wail—as it headed for the city. But then even that faded away.

Ford's face was shocked, incredulous. They'd just taken Dad. He couldn't believe it. And he'd just stood by and let them do it. He couldn't believe that, either.

You couldn't imagine Dad away from the swamp. He hardly ever left it, except to go a few miles up or down the river in his boat. And now he'd been bundled into the back of an ambulance, strapped down, and taken to the city, a place he hated.

Ford gnawed at his lip, trying to stop his tears of anger and frustration. He'd never seen Dad so helpless, so humiliated.

"Gran shouldn't have called them!" he spat out. "Dad was all right! Dad would've gotten better! He would've gotten better here, in the swamp."

Ford stared through the gap where the billboard had been. Before, you could only see the tops of the tallest towers in the city center. Now you could see the whole crowded landscape in between. The rushing traffic, the dazzle off glass and metal, and the concrete tangle of highways made Ford's head spin. Dad was out there somewhere in that roaring confusion. To Ford it felt like his father had been taken prisoner by an evil empire.

And suddenly, Ford couldn't stand it. It was just too overwhelming. Dad had been taken away while he just stood and watched. He went running off into the swamp.

The swamp was steaming, drying out rapidly in the hot afternoon sun. Ford roamed around, hardly knowing where he was going or what he was doing. But there was a logic to his wanderings. He was checking on things. The billboard might have fallen, but other things that were so important to life in the swamp were still there. Mom's angel was in her inlet off Willow Creek—even the flash flood hadn't been able to shift her. Hog, that wily old devil, had somehow ridden out the storm. He looked in a mean mood, though, thrashing about deep in his pool. But he hadn't abandoned them. Swamp Dog wasn't around. Ford wondered again whether the flash flood had drowned him. But then, he tried to comfort himself, you often didn't see Swamp Dog for ages. And suddenly, there he'd be, slinking into the reeds, or nudging up stones with his nose looking for crabs.

Then Ford cried out with delight. He forgot all about Swamp Dog because he'd found their boat. It hadn't been battered to bits. It was still in good shape, high and dry, wedged in a willow tree.

He was wondering how to get it down when Firebird found him. She'd been to the house to get cleaned up, change her clothes, and grab some food.

"Want a sandwich?" she asked him. "Hey, look at the boat!"

Ford crammed the sandwich into his mouth, chewing and talking at the same time.

"It's okay," he said. "How lucky is that? Me and Dad can start trapping eels again straight away."

"What?" Firebird stared at him. "Are you stupid or something? There's no smokery anymore."

"We'll find another one," said Ford. He was suddenly too excited to eat. He threw half his sandwich into the creek.

"There's no money in eel fishing anymore. That guy told you."

"It's just a bad time right now," said Ford, not even looking at her, busy snapping off branches trying to get to the boat. "There'll be good times again soon."

"What's the *matter* with you?" Firebird yelled at him desperately. "Things can't ever be the same. Not *ever.* They lied to us. Gran and Dad both did. About loads of things."

"So what?" said Ford.

At last, he turned and looked at her. Firebird had thought there'd be craziness in his eyes, that he'd finally flipped, unable to handle everything that had happened. But his eyes seemed level and steady—and sane.

Firebird faltered. "What do you mean, *so what?*"

"They were protecting us," said Ford. "I didn't understand it before, but now I do. I mean, it's obvious."

Firebird slumped down on the bank. Deep in the swamp, Hog's bell was ringing. For him, at least, things were back to normal. He was saying, "Hog wants his dinner!"

Ford came and squatted by her on the boggy ground. He started to talk—fast, passionately, as if he'd just had a blinding revelation.

"Okay," he said, "this is how I see it. Things were bad in the eel-fishing business, but they didn't want to worry us. Right? They knew things'd get better again soon. So they thought, *We'll sell Firebird's purses for a bit, make some cash.* What's so wrong with that?"

"They should've told me," insisted Firebird. "Instead of making up stupid lies—all that stuff about keeping them in Gran's cupboard. Why didn't they tell us the truth? We're not *babies* anymore."

Ford had a quick answer for that. "You know what Dad's like," he said. "Proud as anything! He didn't like it, some girlie little handbags keeping the family going. So he kept it all a secret and pretended the money was still coming from eel fishing. And he got Gran to pretend, too."

Firebird frowned. Suddenly, Ford was Dad's champion again. He could explain everything away.

"What about Mom's memorial?" said Firebird, gazing up the creek. "What if they're lying about that, too?"

She thought he'd be outraged at that. That Mom's angel was a secondhand memorial from somebody else's tombstone. Just leftover junk from some old city graveyard. That wasn't respectful at all. Especially when Mom had been such a saintly person.

But Ford just shrugged. He couldn't see the problem with that, either. It was down to Dad's pride again. Firebird didn't understand Trapper like he did.

"So what?" said Ford again. "They just wanted us to think they'd bought something special for Mom. Like Dad said, 'An angel for an angel.' It's not their fault they couldn't afford to get her a brand-new one."

"It's still a *lie*," insisted Firebird.

"It's just what they *wished* could've happened," said Ford. He could forgive Dad and Gran; he could find reasons. Why couldn't Firebird?

"Why are you making such a big deal out of it?" he asked. "Like they're criminals or something?"

And now Firebird was doubting herself again. Was she making a big fuss about nothing? Overreacting? Being too self-righteous? Shouldn't she be able to forgive, like Ford was doing? He made it seem so easy.

Ford said, "They were only trying to do what was best."

Firebird looked at her twin brother with new eyes. Maybe she'd been wrong about him all along. Maybe he was the grown-up one and not her. Why couldn't she be as wise and understanding as he was being?

Then she remembered something else.

"They lied about my name," she told Ford. "Why would they do that?"

Ford stared at her. "What are you talking about?"

"I'm not named after that red car, that Pontiac Firebird ad. I asked the old guy that cleaned the billboard. There was never any Firebird poster up there. He said he could swear to it."

Ford's brow scrunched up, as if even he couldn't explain that one away.

He suddenly turned on her like a goaded animal. "Oh, I don't know!" he yelled. "Who cares about your stupid name? Stop thinking about yourself all the time. It's *Dad* we should be thinking about."

And again, Firebird had to admit to herself that her twin brother had a point.

"Dad should be back here, in the swamp," Ford was muttering. "He'll be all right, once he's back here."

Inside his head, he'd got it all worked out. Dad would get better, they'd put the billboard back up, eel fishing would get through the bad times, start to make money again, and then life would go on as before. Why did Firebird have to make it all so complicated, plant doubts in his mind?

"Let's go and get Dad," said Ford suddenly. "That's the best thing to do."

He looked really happy now that he'd decided. Now he could stop all the talking and take some action.

Firebird stared at him. "Should we?"

She hated it, too, being stuck here, not knowing what was going on or whether Dad was all right. And now she had a new, guilty feeling. After what Ford had said, Firebird was wondering: If Gran and Dad had twisted the truth a bit—even a lot—was that so terrible? They were only trying to protect them, do the best for the family. She wanted to go find them now, this minute, give Gran some hugs, make it up to her for all those cold, suspicious looks.

"We'd have to go to the city," she reminded Ford. "I mean, *right* into the city."

Ford had always boasted, like Trapper, "I'm never going to that place. It's got nothing I need."

But now the city did have something Ford needed. It was holding his dad prisoner. And Ford was desperate to find him.

"So what?" said Ford. "Let's get going. I want to see Dad and tell him I found the boat. Tell him Hog's still here. That everything's fine."

"They said they were taking Dad to the city hospital," said Firebird. She'd seen that name written somewhere.

And then she remembered: It was after she'd set the bird free and looked up at the signpost to find her way back to the plaza.

"I know how to get there," said Firebird. But Ford was already running ahead.

17

GRAN paced the waiting room at the hospital, rubbing her freckled arms up and down, up and down. They'd taken Trapper off somewhere, she didn't know where. No one had been to see her or tell her anything. And she was worrying, too, about how Ford and Firebird were coping back home—the flash flood had done a lot of damage.

"Everything's going wrong at once," muttered Gran, shaking her head. "I never thought the billboard would go, though."

She still found that hard to believe. And it was just another big thing to worry about. If they didn't put it back up pretty quick, all sorts of busybodies would come nosing around the Tuckers' property.

Gran feared the child protection people most of all. They'd probably take the twins away, say Trapper was an unfit parent. For a start, he'd never sent them to school.

"What do they need school for?" he'd say. "Just put ideas in their heads."

Above Gran's head in a corner, a TV yakked. There'd been a woman in there with a whimpering baby when Gran had arrived. But they'd taken her off somewhere. Now Gran was left on her own.

Wish I could turn that thing off, she thought. It was some comedy show, with the audience whooping and cackling like crazy people. But the TV set was mounted high up on a wall.

Gran had never been in a hospital before in her life. The place spooked her with its sickly, disinfectant smells, squeaky rubber floor, and silent people in white coats rushing by.

Maybe they'd forgotten all about her. Down in the swamp Gran was used to being boss. She handled all the information, knew things nobody else knew. She had shaped the Tuckers' family history, invented some parts and left out others. Even Trapper didn't know all her secrets.

She felt guilty about that sometimes, all the deception. But, she told herself, she'd had no other choice. She often wished it was different. As the twins grew up, it was hard keeping track of all the lies—cracks were starting to show. She'd even wondered if Firebird suspected something.

But here in the hospital, Gran had no power. She felt angry, confused, helpless, and scared. All those feelings that Firebird had become so familiar with since she'd unlocked Gran's cupboard.

"Don't even know where they've taken my own son," muttered Gran. "Don't know what's wrong with him, what they're doing to him."

On the wall was a clock. The big hand made a whir and

a click every time it jerked around. Gran had only been in the waiting room for twenty-five minutes, but already it seemed like hours.

It was driving her mad, not knowing. Her whole body itched like there were ants crawling all over it. She felt claustrophobic, cooped up like a chicken.

She stomped over to the window. *It's hotter than hell in here*, she thought. Back in the swamp she was outdoors most of the time, in the fresh air.

"Damn."

Even the window was sealed tight so you couldn't open it. She tried to wrench it open. Gran was a strong woman, used to having things her way.

"Mrs. Tucker? Mrs. Carol-Ann Tucker?"

Gran spun around guiltily, blushing a deep crimson, feeling like a child caught doing something forbidden.

The door of the tiny waiting room had been thrown wide open. A young doctor stood there in a white coat.

Gran nodded, wiping her sweaty hands down her jeans. "That's me."

He came into the room. Gran thought, *He looks about twelve. He can't even be shaving yet.* But he had the power here. Gran knew she had to act polite, respectful, or he might rush away again without telling her anything.

He consulted a clipboard. "Your son is a Mr. John Tucker?" he asked.

Gran felt her mouth go dry. She knew news was coming, but had no idea whether it was good or bad. All she could do was wait until he chose to tell her. He was studying his notes. She wanted to grab him by the throat, shake him and shout, "Tell me, quick!" But she forced herself to stay silent.

"He's got malaria," said the doctor at last.

"What?" said Gran, stunned. "What did you say?"

"Malaria," repeated the young doctor slowly, as if Gran was some poor, ignorant, backwoods woman with no education. "Do you know what that is?"

"But, Doctor—," began Gran.

Then his beeper went off and he whisked away, white coat flying, with a quick "Excuse me" flung back over his shoulder.

Gran's legs felt weak. She slumped down on one of the hard plastic chairs and dragged a hand down over her face. *Malaria*, she thought wonderingly. But how could that be? There were always mosquitoes in the swamp in summer. All of them had got bitten. But none of them had ever caught malaria before. It was true that Trapper got bitten much worse than they did. That he wouldn't use insect repellent or cover up. He'd brag about it, saying it was sissy stuff. He even played a kind of game. He'd let mosquitoes land on his arm, then squash them when they were busy sucking his blood.

But no matter how much Trapper got bitten, that didn't explain it.

Nobody gets malaria in this country, thought Gran, shaking her head. *They get it in Africa, places like that.*

Gran stood up. She couldn't stay in this tiny room a second longer, worrying herself stupid. She had to go and see Trapper, find out what was happening. But what if they didn't let her see him?

She thought, *Just let them try and stop me.*

Gran stormed out into the corridor, ready for trouble. She couldn't stand it, being kept in the dark, treated as if she had no right to know.

She looked around for someone in a white coat. "Where are you keeping my son?" was going to be her first question.

Then she saw a girl who looked like Firebird, standing alone farther down the corridor, under a sign that read: WARD SEVEN.

At first it gave her a jolt. But then Gran told herself, *You silly old fool, it can't be her.* Firebird was back in the swamp. *They've just got the same red hair,* Gran decided. Besides, Firebird would never come to the city. Not in a million years. She'd been warned off it too many times.

But then the girl turned around. And it *was* Firebird. Gran went rushing up to her. "What are you doing here? I told you to stay put." But she couldn't be angry. She was too relieved to see a familiar face.

"Shhh!" said Firebird, putting a finger to her lips. "Ford's in there, with Dad." She jerked a thumb behind her.

"Let's go in then," said Gran, about to barge through the ward doors.

But Firebird said, "No, Gran, you can't. They said only one visitor at a time. We've got to wait until Ford comes out."

Gran forced herself to take deep breaths and calm down. "How'd you and Ford get here?" she demanded suddenly.

A nurse rushed by and shot Gran a disapproving glance, as if loud talking wasn't allowed.

Gran sighed. "This damn place," she whispered. "It gives me the creeps. Come back in here."

She led Firebird back into the waiting room. They perched on the hard plastic chairs while the TV burbled away above them.

"Me and Ford came through the storm drains," said Firebird. "And the subways. We followed the signs. We came up in the elevator."

All sorts of alarm bells were ringing in Gran's head. Firebird didn't seem panicked by the city. She looked confident, proud of knowing the way. Gran had a sudden, shocking thought: *Has Firebird been to the city before?*

She can't have, Gran decided. *I'd know about it.* In the swamp, Gran was the keeper of secrets. People didn't keep secrets from her.

"Did you lock up the house?" she asked Firebird. Now that the billboard was gone, who knows who'd come snooping around? Especially without Trapper to chase them off.

But then all other worries were driven out of her head because Firebird said, "We talked to a nurse. She told us where Dad was."

"Did she tell you anything else about your dad?" urged Gran. "Think now."

Firebird shook her head. "No."

Gran frowned. "Never tell you nothing in this place, do they?"

Firebird put out a hand, placed it gently over Gran's

big, knotted hand, the skin sandpapery rough from all the hard work she did.

"Don't worry, Gran," she said. "Everything'll be all right. Dad'll be all right."

And Gran looked really grateful for some comfort.

And, in the next few minutes, all Firebird's anguished doubts and suspicions seemed unimportant. It was a big relief to be friendly with Gran again; it had been torment not to trust her. And Firebird badly needed Gran's strength and protection, especially now that the billboard had fallen.

Ford was right, thought Firebird. Gran and Trapper had only been trying to do what was best. And she, Firebird, had been too harsh and unforgiving. Firebird patted Gran's hand. It felt good to be back in the family fold again.

A nurse poking her head around the door broke up their private moment.

"Mrs. Tucker?" she demanded. "Mrs. Carol-Ann Tucker?"

Gran looked up. "Message for you here," said the nurse. "Left at reception."

She thrust a folded piece of paper into Gran's hand. Then she was gone. Gran stared at the paper, baffled. "Now what's this all about?"

She unfolded it and smoothed it out on her knee. There was a long silence while she read it, over and over again.

Finally, she whispered something. It sounded like "Dear god." The paper fluttered to the ground. Gran and Firebird dived for it at the same time. Firebird got there first.

"Don't you read that!" snapped Gran. "It's not for you!"

But it was too late. Firebird had already picked it up. She'd seen what was written on the paper.

I'm back, the message said, *if you need help*. Then there was a telephone number. And it was signed with a name: *Loreal*.

18

AT FIRST Ford had been traumatized, seeing Dad in this alien place, all hooked up to drips. Trapper was propped up on three pillows, his eyes closed, his cheekbones flushed pink.

Ford had one anguished thought: *What have they done to him?*

They'd put him in a white hospital gown, like he was a baby. Trapper was a little, wiry guy and the gown didn't fit. It was made for someone much bigger. He was nearly lost inside it. That upset Ford almost more than anything else.

Trapper was in a side room on his own. Ford could hear the sounds of the ward, nurses' voices, and the clattering of trays and trolleys. But in here it was strangely hushed. It was shadowy, too, because someone had half closed the blinds. No one came in, or even put their heads around the door. Ford fidgeted on the chair.

Then Dad opened his eyes.

The drugs they'd used on him had brought his temperature down. He was out of the danger zone for the moment. And he wasn't delirious anymore. He felt a lot more like his old self.

"Come here," he croaked at Ford.

Ford's heart leaped with joy. He sprang over to the bed. "Dad! Dad! You okay?"

"Be a lot better when I get out of this place," said Trapper. "Look in that locker, son. Give me my clothes."

"But, Dad, you can't, Dad," whispered Ford, looking over his shoulder in case someone might be listening. "They won't let you."

"Who won't let me?" said Trapper. He was desperate to get back to the swamp. Not just because that was where he belonged—like Ford, he thought it was the only place he would get well again—but because the swamp needed him there to defend it.

"I heard them talking," grinned Trapper. "They thought I was asleep, but I fooled 'em."

Ford brightened up and grinned back. This was the Trapper he knew and loved. The Trapper who never let anything defeat him.

"It was some guy from the Public Health Department," said Trapper, "and a doctor. Anyway, this public health guy says, 'We think a new strain of mosquitoes have started breeding in the swamp area just outside the city.' And the doctor says, 'That's very worrying.'"

"Mosquitoes?" interrupted Ford, frowning. "I don't get it, Dad. There've always been mosquitoes in the swamp."

"Yeah," said Trapper. "But now some of 'em are malaria-carrying ones from Africa. That's what this guy said. He talked about global warming. He said now that the world's heating up, these mosquitoes are breeding in places they never did before."

"Do you believe that, Dad?" asked Ford.

"Nah," said Trapper. "It's just another excuse to get rid of the swamp. They've been trying to do it for years. This guy says, 'To protect the city, we're going to have to drain the swamp. Destroy the mosquitoes' breeding grounds.'"

"Drain the swamp?" said Ford, horrified. "They won't really do that, will they, Dad?"

"Over my dead body," said Trapper.

He ripped the bandage off the back of his hand and pulled out the needle that was pumping drugs into his body. Blood spurted out all over the sheets until Trapper pressed the vein to close it up and tied the bandage back on again with his teeth.

"Now hand me my clothes," said Trapper, swinging his legs out of the bed. When his feet touched the floor he staggered and sank back on the bed.

"I'm all right," he said to Ford.

Ford had to help him into his jeans and T-shirt. He was wobbly on his legs, but Ford tried to ignore that. Dad would be all right once they got home.

Ford said, "So what's supposed to be wrong with you, Dad?"

"They said I've got malaria," said Trapper.

"Oh," said Ford, his mind clicking over furiously. He hadn't connected all that stuff about African mosquitoes with Dad's illness.

"Don't believe 'em, son," said Trapper. "Like I just

said, it's an excuse to get their hands on the swamp. Like that FWS guy with the fish eagle that's supposed to be there. There's no malaria-carrying mosquitoes. Just like there's no fish eagle."

Dad was talking a lot, much more than normal. His eyes were oddly bright. The flush on his face was deepening from pink to crimson.

"They kept saying, 'You got any connection with the swamp, Mr. Tucker?' Course I just looked dumb. So they still don't know we're there. And you can count on your gran; she won't breathe a word . . ."

As Trapper was sneaking toward the door, Ford suddenly realized, *He doesn't know that the billboard's down.* Dad was totally out of it when the ambulance took him away. He had no idea that the Tuckers' lives weren't a secret anymore.

But Ford didn't plan to tell him now. Ford still believed that somehow, even without the billboard, his dad would make everything all right.

Trapper winked at him like a conspirator. Ford grinned back. It was like it was before, when he and Dad had worked side by side, trusting each other.

"Go and see if there's any of those nurses around," said Trapper. "And if there isn't, we'll make a run for it."

"What about Gran and Firebird?" said Ford.

"Firebird's here, too?" A cloud crossed Trapper's face, as if he didn't like Firebird being in the city. Trapper had always been terrified that the city would claim his daughter. After all, as he'd often told her, Firebird was so much like her mother.

But then Trapper seemed to forget about that, as if he could only keep his mind on one thing at once. "No time to find them," he said. "Me and you, we've got to get back to the swamp. Stop them getting their thieving hands on it."

Ford wasn't sure who "them" was. Did Trapper mean the FWS or the public health people? But he said, "Right, Dad!" anyhow. He could feel excitement and pride fizzing inside him. He was all psyched up again, feeling heroic. He and Dad wouldn't let anyone, whoever they were, lay a finger on the swamp.

"Okay, Dad," whispered Ford, peering into the ward. "It's clear." There were no nurses in sight, just a couple of sick people shuffling around in dressing gowns.

Hang on, there's one, thought Ford, his heart giving a nervous flutter. But she was busy taking a patient's blood pressure.

Ford was trying hard not to snigger as he and Dad crept across the ward. It felt like they were sneaking out right under that nurse's nose!

Ford couldn't help saying, once they were clear of the ward, "Wonder where Firebird's gone?" He'd left her waiting outside.

"She'll be with Gran somewhere," said Trapper. "Let's go before they see us. I don't want them back at the swamp. Not yet. They're better off out of the way."

Ford couldn't make much sense of that. But he said, "Okay, Dad," again, and nodded wisely as if he understood.

It was easier than Ford thought it would be to get out of the building. No one challenged them or even gave them a second glance. The place was swarming with people on different errands: medical staff rushing around, patients going for X-rays, visitors carrying flowers.

"We'll take the elevator," said Ford. He was relieved when no one followed them in.

"What time is it?" asked Trapper, shivering in a corner as the elevator swished down. "You lose all sense of time in this place."

"I don't know. Five o'clock?" guessed Ford. "Six o'clock?"

"Good," said Trapper. "We've got three, maybe four hours of daylight left."

"What are you going to do, Dad?"

"You'll see," said Trapper. "You'll see." Dad's voice sounded uncompromising. Like it was time to take a stand. Ford wished he didn't look so strange and scary—his eyes gleaming fanatically, his voice fevered and urgent.

He also didn't like how, as they walked across the lobby, Dad's legs were as wobbly as a toddler's. But getting out of the building seemed to revive Trapper and give him some strength back.

"Which way now?" he said, staring at the rush-hour traffic chaos.

Ford stared around, too. On the way here, when he and Firebird had surfaced into the plaza, she'd pointed out some landmarks.

"That's the shop over there where my purses are. And see that tallest building? I've been right to the top of it. I smashed the searchlight. I smashed it good."

"You did *what?*" He just couldn't imagine that at all. Firebird right up there, almost in the clouds, doing something like that. "Come on," he'd said, "you're kidding me."

But then she'd said it again. "I smashed the searchlight. The one that killed all the pretty birds."

Then she'd plunged into the crowd. And Ford had hurried after, scared of losing sight of her. But he'd noticed how proud she sounded. Like she knew her way around, like she'd left her mark on this place.

And then, just down the street, near some dusty, drooping trees, she'd said, "This is where I set the bird free."

At the time, Ford hadn't taken much notice of anything she told him. He'd been too overwhelmed by the noise, the traffic, the city's manic pace. He'd never seen such crowds, even on market day in Hook Bay. And he used to imagine, staring from the swamp, that the city was peopleless, that it ran on its own.

But now that the first shock of the city was over, he was remembering what Firebird had told him. And his eyes searched upward, to that tallest tower where she said she'd smashed the searchlight. Had she really done that?

From here, Ford couldn't see any smashed searchlight. But he did see two hawks circling around the top. Unsettled by Firebird's attack, they still hadn't gone back to their favorite daytime perch.

"See the hawks, Dad?" said Ford. "That's where we want to be."

He wasn't sure if he could find the way back through the subways and storm drains. But, first things first, at least the hawks would lead them to the plaza.

Trapper's eyes focused hungrily on the hawks, soaring high above the city streets, as though they were a sign of freedom.

"Come on, son," said Trapper. "We've got things to do."

19

FORD said, "I don't think it's that way, Dad."

"Which way then?" demanded Trapper, his eyes burning with a spooky glow in the subway's gloom.

Trapper was so desperate to get back to the swamp that he seemed hyperactive. His body twitched. He was scratching at the back of his hand where the needle had gone in to feed him malaria-busting drugs.

Ford didn't want to let on. But he had the dreadful suspicion that he was lost, that he'd taken a wrong turn somewhere. All these white-tiled passages looked the same, smelled the same, of pee. They were all eerily empty and echoing. This far from the city center, there wasn't a single pedestrian to be seen.

But someone was down here, in these forgotten tunnels. From one of the side passages came a groan and then a whimper.

"Hey!" shouted Trapper as he peered down the side passage. "Who's there?" It wasn't lit. But there was a feeble, gray light filtering down from above through some kind of grill. It was enough to see by.

Trapper saw a huddle of rags in a nest of sleeping bags. He saw a shuddering, skinny dog on a rope.

"Swamp Dog," said Trapper, stumbling up to him, crouching down. "What are you doing here, boy?"

Swamp Dog had fled the storm surge, escaping by the skin of his teeth, only to be collared by his former master as he slunk through the tunnels.

Swamp Dog was tied by a rope to a hairy ankle. Trapper bent down to free him. Suddenly, the rags woke up and were flung back. Trapper saw a face scrunched up in rage and bewilderment, eyes like blue diamonds. Trapper backed away, into the shadows.

A thick, slurred voice said, "You trying to steal my dog?"

As the man struggled to his feet, empty vodka bottles clinked and rolled away. He lurched toward Trapper. Trapper was swaying, too, but he didn't back off any farther.

The man aimed a kick at Swamp Dog. It connected with his skinny ribs and Swamp Dog yelped, then ran to hide behind Ford.

"Shouldn't have done that," said Trapper.

His voice seemed calm, even friendly. But Ford could hear the trembling edge to it, the barely suppressed tension and he knew it was a dangerous sign. Dad had sounded like that before he'd gone berserk and smashed the solar panel. He was breathing heavily, too.

"Leave it, Dad," said Ford, his voice urgent, pleading. "Come on, we've got to go. We've got things to do, remember?"

Ford held on to Swamp Dog by the rope around his neck so he didn't run. "Swamp Dog knows the way back," said Ford.

But Trapper wasn't listening. All his attention was on the man. He was much bigger than Trapper, taller and heavier. And he was growling like an angry grizzly bear.

"Come on, Dad," urged Ford, hearing the panic in his own voice. Dad was in no condition to fight.

"Come on then," Trapper invited the man. He yanked his lighter out of his pocket, sparked it, and let the tiny flame flicker. Then he began waving it to and fro, to and fro, in front of the man's eyes, as if to hypnotize him. "Come on."

The man let out a roar. Then he charged at Trapper, arms out to grab him by the throat. But he was slow and clumsy. Trapper had time to snap his lighter shut and slip it back in his pocket. Then he sidestepped, put out one foot, and tripped the man up. He went sprawling onto the ground, looking really surprised, like he didn't know why he was there.

Ford laughed at the astonished expression on the man's face. "Cool, Dad!" he said, weak with relief that Trapper hadn't come off any worse. "You fixed him good! Now let's go."

But then he stopped laughing. Because Trapper didn't leave it there. He moved in on the man, kicking him in the legs, the kidneys, through his thick overcoat. He was too weak to do any damage. But the man yelled out, covered his head with his hands. "That'll teach you!" raved Trapper. "Shouldn't kick dogs. Shouldn't go around kicking dogs. Don't you ever, *never* show your face in my swamp again!"

"Dad!" said Ford. "That's enough, Dad. Leave him. He's drunk."

Ford grabbed Trapper's arm. Trapper looked around at him savagely like Ford was a stranger and he was going to start on him next. Then recognition flared in his eyes.

"Dad," said Ford. "Please."

Trapper looked down at the man at his feet, trying to crawl back to his sleeping bag, as if he'd never seen him before. He put his hand to his head, swayed, and stared around at the tunnel walls.

Then he said, "Where are we, for god's sake? What the hell did I just do?"

"Come on, Dad," coaxed Ford gently. "Let's go home."

Swamp Dog was already pulling on the rope, taking them in the right direction.

"Come on, Dad. It'll be all right when we get home. It'll be all right."

Trapper nodded silently and let himself be led away, as if he was the child now and Ford was the parent. As he staggered along, he kept shaking his head, as if he still didn't understand what had just happened.

But once they got through the storm drains and Trapper saw the billboard was gone, he seemed to recover all his furious energy.

"We've got to move fast," he said to Ford. "They'll be coming soon. Nothing to stop 'em now."

Ford nodded. "Okay, Dad, okay," he said. But he was full of uncertainty. Had Dad finally cracked with all the threats to the swamp or was it his sickness talking? But Ford pushed his doubts aside. He couldn't let his dad down. And Trapper's feverish activity, the purpose blazing in his eyes, drove them both along.

Trapper seemed to have the strength of ten men. And he seemed to know exactly what he was doing, as if he'd already had it all planned out in his head. Even though his half-mad mutterings didn't make much sense: "Knew it would come to this one day. They pushed me and pushed me, well they're not going to get this place that easy . . ."

As soon as he smelled the swamp, Swamp Dog was straining at the rope, whimpering to be free. Ford untied him and he shot off to hide in the reeds, as if he'd had enough of humans to last him his whole doggy lifetime.

They were in the yard now and Trapper was hurling debris aside to get to the little shack where they stored fuel for the boat. He wrenched the door open. The fuel cans, high on a shelf inside, hadn't been touched by the flood. Trapper grabbed a couple.

Ford was thrilled. He actually believed for a few seconds that normality had come back. He told himself, *We're going out eel fishing again.*

He said, "I found the boat, Dad. It's wedged in a tree, but I think it's okay."

"Good," said Trapper. "We're going to need it."

Ford laughed uneasily. "Course we'll need it, Dad. Can't go eel fishing without it."

Trapper shot him a surprised glance that meant "Who said anything about eel fishing?" Then he ordered Ford, "Grab a couple more of those cans."

The outboard doesn't take this much fuel, thought Ford. Now those alarm bells were really ringing in his brain. He tried to ignore their shrill warnings. He went wading through the boggy yard after Trapper, carrying the cans.

"Where are we going, Dad?" asked Ford.

He thought Dad should go to bed and get some rest. He looked like a dead man walking.

When Trapper didn't answer, Ford said, "Should I show you where the boat's at? We could get it down easy, now there's two of us."

Trapper was trudging ahead. He turned around, his face shiny with sweat. For a second he stared blankly at Ford, as if he'd forgotten who he was. Then he seemed to shudder himself awake.

"First," he said, "we're going to check on something."

There was already a grayness about the swamp. Things looked fuzzy, indistinct. It must be later than Ford thought. But the city lights hadn't been switched on yet. So maybe it was just mist, rolling in from the river, sliding up all the creeks. It was deathly still, too, after the big storm, as though the swamp itself had stopped breathing. The wind had dropped completely.

Ford was bursting with questions. But he tried to keep quiet, like he always did when working with Dad in the swamp. Even though everything about this scary little setup screamed at him, *We're not going eel catching. Dad's acting crazy. He doesn't know what he's doing.*

But still, against all the evidence, he tried to keep the faith. *Don't get panicky. Dad will make everything all right.*

The floodwater had drained away really fast from the swamp—the paths were already dry underfoot. As they turned onto the path that ran alongside Willow Creek,

Ford suddenly thought, *I know where Dad's heading.* He was going to check on Mom's memorial, to make sure the flood hadn't carried it away.

It gave Ford a warm feeling, that Mom's memorial was the first thing Dad wanted to see when he got home. As if Mom, even though she was dead, was a treasured part of the family. As if the Tucker family bonds still held strong.

Ford broke his silence so Dad could be reassured. "I already checked, Dad. The angel's fine."

But Trapper gave one scornful glance at the angel as she stared up, with those wide, empty eyes, through the weeds.

"Huh," muttered Trapper. "You certainly weren't no angel."

"What?" said Ford. "What did you say, Dad?"

But Trapper had already stomped on.

"Boat's just down there, Dad," Ford called after him. "Want me to show you?"

But Trapper didn't stop or turn back, so Ford had to chase after him, still lugging the heavy fuel cans.

All sorts of weird things were coming out of Trapper's mouth. He was cursing to himself, mumbling like a wizard casting a spell.

It's not his fault, thought Ford, *he's sick.*

Dad was stopping now, putting down the gasoline cans and slumping against a tree.

Ford went rushing up. "You all right, Dad? Can I carry them for you?"

But Trapper pushed him away. "Stop fussing. I'm okay." He picked up the cans and staggered on again.

And, for the first time, it occurred to Ford, *Maybe Dad's sicker than I thought. Maybe he'd be better off back in the hospital.* But he immediately dismissed that as a treacherous idea.

And now Ford knew where Dad was really going. He was going to check on Hog. Ford was about to say, "Hog's still here, too, Dad. I meant to tell you." But a sudden, ominous thought stopped him. *Why wasn't Hog ringing his bell?* No one had given him his dinner. The old tyrant should be ringing his bell like crazy for someone to come and feed him.

It was eerie down at Hog's pool. The mist was drifting over it. Then, out in the swamp, Ford saw a ball of blue fire. It hovered, ghostly and glowing, just above the reeds.

"Witch light, Dad," said Ford.

But Trapper was too busy staring into Hog's pool.

Ford had never believed Gran's stories—that the lights were sent by some old witch to trap children. Gran had scared Firebird stupid, but not him. So why was he shuddering now? Why couldn't he shake off the thought that this was some kind of evil omen?

Then Trapper said, "Hog's gone."

"What?" said Ford. He threw himself down full length by the pool, staring in. He tried to convince himself he could see Hog, his pale coils writhing and glimmering down in the shadowy depths. But it was only a trick of the light. And if Hog had been there, he would have been up here by now, in a mean mood, his teeth gnashing, his little red eyes glinting because he'd been kept waiting for so long for his dinner.

"Well, that settles it," said Trapper, getting up wearily from beside the pool, grasping the fuel cans. "The old bugger knows when it's all over. So should we."

And now Ford really was panicking. *What was Dad planning to do?* Trapper's eyes were wilder now, even more so than when he'd wrecked the solar panel, or kicked that poor, drunken guy in the subway.

Then Ford yelled out, "Look, Dad! There's Hog. Look, I can see him. Look, there."

Ford pointed, his hand shaking. It was Hog all right; you couldn't mistake him. The great white eel, king of the swamp, was gliding like some mythical beast through the sundews. But he was going in the opposite direction, away from his pool, toward the river.

Ford couldn't help it. He cried out, "Hog, come back," as if Hog would obey a human voice and come to heel, like a dog.

A frightening calm seemed to have come over Trapper. As if he'd half expected this to happen. And now that it had, he had nothing else to lose. "He's gone, son," he said to Ford.

"No, he isn't," insisted Ford, as frenzied as Trapper had been a minute ago. "He's just on a little hunting trip. You'll see, Dad. He'll be back soon, I bet."

Trapper put an arm around Ford's shoulder, tried to comfort him. It was the first time he'd ever done anything like that—Trapper wasn't a hugging kind of person. But Ford was too distraught to notice.

"He'll be back soon, Dad, when he's caught his dinner."

Trapper shook his head. His voice sounded sad, but strangely accepting. "We won't see him again. He's gone back to the Sargasso Sea where he came from."

Hog had lived for over sixty years in the swamp. But now he was migrating back, thousands and thousands of miles to the warm sea where he was born. He was going back to breed and die. It was a long and mystical journey. Who knew what was pulling him back now, at this precise moment?

But Trapper thought he knew. "It's all over for us Tuckers here," he told Ford.

"No, Dad," said Ford, pleading, close to tears. "Don't say that."

Trapper's reply was kind, but uncompromising. "Sorry, son, I can't say any different." But then he added, "Don't worry. We're not going to go quietly."

Trapper picked up the gasoline cans. After being so agitated he seemed almost serene now, as if he knew what he had to do. As if Hog leaving the swamp had somehow sanctioned his course of action.

"Now," he said to Ford, "show me where that boat's at."

Ford led Dad to the boat, hurrying through the reed beds, alongside Whiskey Creek, back to Willow Creek. The swamp had been ripped apart, rearranged by the storm. Its whole geography was different. Some creeks were choked with debris. Others, silted up for years, were now free-running. Some islands had disappeared, new ones made.

And it stank, too, of dead fish and raw sewage from the city that had been washed up by the storm surge. *Phew,* thought Ford, his face wrinkling up in disgust. He hardly recognized the place as home anymore.

"There she is," said Ford, putting down his fuel cans— they were making his arm muscles ache. He couldn't understand why they were hauling them around like this.

Dad put his cans down, too, and stared up at the boat left high and dry in the willow.

"Think the outboard's okay, Dad?" asked Ford.

Trapper shook his head. "Can't tell until we get her down. There's no fuel leaking, though."

After a few minutes of hectic work, smashing and splintering the branches that trapped her, the boat came sliding free, and splashed into the creek.

"She's floating!" said Ford. It was about time they had some good luck.

Trapper moored the boat, inspected it for damage.

"Would you believe it," he said to Ford, shaking his head in admiration. "Still watertight. That's a good boat. Worth all our hard work, eh, son, to buy her?"

Ford felt a glow of pride at Trapper's praise. But at the same time—he couldn't help it—another subversive thought sneaked into his head. *It wasn't our hard work that bought that boat. It was Firebird's.*

He crushed that thought immediately. He was prepared to forgive Dad everything. He didn't want to call Dad to account or challenge him. And, even if he'd wanted to, this wasn't the right time.

Every second, Ford kept expecting Dad to collapse. But, shaking and sweating at the same time, he somehow kept going.

Now he was in the boat, trying out the engine. The engine coughed once, twice, then snarled to life.

Good, thought Ford. *We're getting out of here.*

Ever since Dad had been taken away to the city hospital, Ford had been convinced that he'd only get better back in the swamp. But now he was beginning to wish that he could get Dad away from here—to the fresh air and the wide, breezy spaces of the open river. As if that might somehow clear Dad's mind, give him back his reason. Because Dad's reason seemed to have gone AWOL. Down in the boat, he was laughing to himself. And that laugh chilled Ford's blood. It was sinister, almost inhuman.

"Let 'em come," muttered Trapper. "Let 'em all come."

Dad was climbing out of the boat again, staggering back up the bank. So they weren't going to head for the open river. It looked like they were staying put. Ford knew now that it wasn't eel trapping that Dad had in mind.

"What are we going to do, Dad?" Ford asked him.

Carefully, as if every bone in his body ached, Trapper lowered himself to the foot of the willow tree, resting his back against it. He felt in his jeans pockets for his lighter and cigarettes. Only one cigarette left—he lit it with shaky hands.

"Dad, did you hear me?" Ford was pleading. Trapper stared up at his son with burning eyes, as if he'd forgotten again that he was there.

"What do we do now, Dad?" asked Ford.

Trapper stretched out his legs and sighed. He seemed almost peaceful. "Now," he told Ford, "we wait."

20

"So is Mom still alive?" Firebird demanded.

Her fists were so clenched up, so tense, that the note from Loreal she still held was squeezed into a tight little ball.

In the hospital waiting room, Gran shifted uncomfortably on her plastic chair.

Gran had spent years telling stories about Loreal. Some were true, some half true; but most were barefaced lies. With some of them, even Gran had forgotten whether they'd happened or not. But now, faced with that one simple question, "Is Mom still alive?" Gran looked pinned down, cornered. She stared helplessly at Firebird, her mind whirling frantically, as if she was trying to invent yet another story to get herself off the hook.

But then Firebird warned her, like a stern parent, "Don't tell me any more lies. I'm sick of them."

And suddenly Gran gave up, surrendered to the truth. She was sick of lies, too. They were too much hard work. And lately, as Firebird and Ford grew up, the lies she'd told, and was telling every day, bothered Gran more and more. She was just too weary to invent any more, to keep the illusion going. Especially now that she could see their lives in the swamp crumbling around them.

"Yes," said Gran. "She's still alive."

And with those few words, you could almost hear that elaborate structure of stories about Loreal shatter and come crashing down.

Firebird gave a huge sigh, as if at last she'd come to the end of a long journey. It was a big relief for Gran, too. Except now that she'd finally confessed the truth, she knew there'd be a big price to pay. What would Trapper say when he found out she'd told the secret?

He'll go crazy, thought Gran. *Absolutely crazy.*

And what about Ford and Firebird? Would they ever trust her again? Looking at Firebird's face, a mixture of wonder, hurt, and bewilderment, Gran was slowly realizing what an unforgivable thing she and Trapper had done.

In the tiny, airless waiting room, a game show burbled on over their heads.

"I'm going to switch that damn thing off," announced Gran, glaring up at the TV. She stood on a chair to reach it. But all the controls had been removed; you couldn't even change channels. Defeated, Gran sat down. She put a hand to her spinning head.

I don't feel too good, she thought.

Firebird was struggling to cope, too. The blinding revelation about Mom had left her stunned at first. Now all sorts of feelings were besieging her. She was angry, she wanted to know *why*. Why had Gran and Dad deceived her all these years? But that wasn't her first priority. What she wanted now, *immediately*, was to know all about Mom. Every single detail. But she didn't want to hear it from Gran's mouth. Gran had told too many lies in the past.

Firebird unfolded her fist and smoothed out Loreal's message.

"I'm going to call her," she said suddenly, springing up from her chair.

"Wait," said Gran.

Firebird shot Gran a fierce, defiant look. "You're not going to stop me!"

"No," said Gran, "I promise I'm not going to stop you."

She fumbled in her pocket and, to show she meant it, thrust some coins at Firebird. "Here, you'll need money for the phone. But just sit down, only for a second, please," Gran begged.

Impatiently, Firebird perched on the edge of a chair, like a wild bird ready for flight.

"I want to tell you about your mother," said Gran. "Things you should know before you call her."

"How do I know they're not lies again?" demanded Firebird, ready to leap up.

"I won't lie, I swear. It's the truth this time." Gran sounded sincere and humble, but Firebird had been deceived so often she wanted double reassurance.

"*Promise* me you're telling the truth. She really is alive, isn't she? Because I couldn't stand it," said Firebird, "if you told me she was dead after all."

Gran had the grace to look ashamed. "Course she's alive," she said. "Who do you think wrote that?" She nodded toward the piece of paper in Firebird's hand. "Though heaven knows how she knew we were here, at the hospital. I haven't told her. I never even knew she was back."

"Where's she been?" asked Firebird.

It was one of a hundred questions crowding her mind, jostling to be first out of her mouth.

"Oh, she's been away," said Gran vaguely.

Firebird flashed her a suspicious look. When Gran got woolly like that she was usually hiding something. Hadn't Gran learned her lesson yet? Didn't she know that Firebird was wiser now, not so easy to fool?

Firebird's scorching look made Gran falter and think again. She might not have learned yet how much Firebird had changed. But she had realized something—that she owed Firebird the truth. And she wanted to give it, even here in this drab little hospital waiting room, as if she couldn't wait to unburden herself.

"Look," she told Firebird, "this is how it happened. I'm not trying to make excuses or anything. I know me and your dad shouldn't have done it . . ."

But even as she said this, Gran was thinking, *Trapper won't be doing any apologizing.* Trapper had never had any doubts about pretending Loreal was dead. He'd always been 100 percent certain that it was the right thing to do, for the sake of the children. "Better for them to think she's dead," Trapper had said, after he'd destroyed all her photos, "than for them to know the truth."

Gran sighed. She hardly knew where to begin. There

was so much Firebird didn't know and when she did, she probably wouldn't understand. Best not to tell Firebird all at once. It would be too much for her to handle. Best to tell her piece by piece.

So Gran said, "I'll tell you about your mom when she was little."

Even as she was craning forward to listen, Firebird had the uneasy feeling that she was being patronized. That this could be another of Gran's stories meant to bewitch and deceive her. And when Gran started, "You and your mom are a lot alike," Firebird's heart sank.

She thought, *Oh no, here we go again.* She'd heard all this before. How they were both good, dutiful girls. How they both loved the swamp so much and had never wanted to roam.

But Gran was saying something different. Firebird listened, her astonishment growing with every word.

"Loreal used to sit by the billboard," said Gran, "staring at them posters, getting ideas in her head. Restless little thing, right from being small. Used to talk your head off! And she was artistic, too, good at making things."

"Did she make purses, like me?" asked Firebird eagerly.

Gran said, "No, she didn't do that. But she used to make herself these crazy outfits, parade around the swamp in 'em. I remember this dress she made—out of some scraps of red stuff, all covered in red feathers."

Firebird couldn't help interrupting. "Did you go to the city to get feathers for *her*, too?"

Gran gave her a sharp look that said, "So you know about that!" Then she told Firebird, "No, someone else gave her those feathers. I never started going to the city until years later. After Loreal ran away there."

"Mom ran away to the city?" said Firebird, stunned. "But I thought she loved the swamp. I thought she never wanted to leave."

Gran nodded, tight-lipped. "Yeah, well, that's how Trapper wanted her to be—a nice, quiet, swamp-loving girl. But that wasn't Loreal. She wasn't like that at all. Only Trapper wouldn't see it—"

"But I don't understand," Firebird butted in again. "If Mom didn't die when I was born, why can't I remember her?"

The only face Firebird ever had in her mind when she thought of Mom was the blank, beautiful face of the stone angel.

"Because she went away to the city," said Gran, "when you and Ford were just babies."

That opened up a whole new nightmare for Firebird. The joy she'd felt in discovering Mom was still alive was suddenly squashed flat.

"She just left us?" said Firebird. "Just went off and *left* us?" She couldn't believe it. Angels aren't supposed to do that.

"It wasn't like that," said Gran.

But she looked really uncomfortable. She was struggling to find words to explain it. But she'd spent so much time building myths around Loreal's memory that the truth was hard to disentangle.

Finally, like a diver taking a plunge into a freezing river, Gran said, "I told her to go."

"What?" said Firebird, not sure she'd heard right. "What did you say?"

"I told her to go," repeated Gran.

"Why did you do that?" Firebird's voice sounded so lost, so hopelessly confused, that it was pitiful.

Gran sighed. She had almost no hope that Firebird would understand. Loreal had been only sixteen when she'd had the twins. She and Trapper hadn't been married. But she'd been sort of promised to Trapper since she was a little girl. Her future was mapped out: Stay in the swamp with Trapper, have his kids, and help him in the eel-fishing business.

"It was driving her mad, cooped up in the swamp," said Gran, desperately anxious to explain. "She never truly belonged there. She and Trapper weren't suited. Not at all. I told her I'd look after the twins. She had to get away."

Gran had been worried about Loreal's sanity, especially after she'd had the babies. That she'd kill herself if she couldn't escape any other way. Drown herself in one of the creeks . . .

"Your dad never knew I told her to go," said Gran. "That I helped her out with money until she found a job. That I saw her afterward, in the city. Told her how you and Ford were getting on. He never knew any of that."

"But why didn't she come back to see us?"

"You know why," said Gran. "Because your dad decided it was best if you and Ford thought she was dead."

"But *you* told us she was dead, too," protested Firebird wildly. "It wasn't just Dad! Why'd *you* say that?"

Gran swayed on her chair. She felt terrible—she could

hardly carry on with this truth-telling session. And the bit they'd got to was the hardest for her to explain, even to herself.

Why had she colluded with Trapper when he'd lied about Loreal, made her out to be some kind of saint, with her own angel statue to honor her memory? Why had she backed him up all the way, made his ridiculous lies seem convincing with her stories?

Gran stared helplessly at Firebird. Whatever she said, she knew it wasn't going to be good enough.

"I couldn't let your dad down again," she told Firebird. "Trapper's my son. And I'd gone behind his back, betrayed him, helped Loreal to leave. I was the only one who could help her," insisted Gran. "By then, the Evanses had moved on, left her behind with us, and they were a worthless, ignorant bunch anyway—never understood her the way I did. But if Trapper ever knew what I did," said Gran, shaking her head. "If he *ever* found out . . ."

"But what about us?" Firebird demanded. "What about me and Ford? Left with no mom?"

"You never wanted for anything, did you?" snapped Gran, as if she'd suddenly lost patience. She wanted to say, "Loreal would've been dead for *real* if she'd stayed. We'd have found her one morning, in one of the creeks."

With her red dress on. That had been Gran's nightmare at the time. Finding Loreal one morning, drowned, floating down one of the creeks with that dress on, all the feathers fanning out around her like red seaweed.

But some truths are too harsh to tell, too unbearable to hear. So Gran sighed, tried to soften her voice. "I know it's hard. But you've got to be very grown-up, try to understand how it was. Your mom was only sixteen, not much older than you—"

Then, startled, Gran broke off and stared at the waiting-room door. It had just burst open and there was a crowd of doctors and nurses looking in.

"He's not in here," one said. And they were rushing off again when Gran said, "What's up?"

One of the nurses stayed behind to answer. "A patient's missing—he's not in his room."

"Who?" said Gran. The nurse looked wary, like it was none of Gran's business. But then she said, "A Mr. John Tucker."

"That's my son," said Gran.

The nurse said, "Oh, I didn't realize."

"Where's my brother?" Firebird was asking. "He was visiting Dad."

The nurse shrugged, shook her head. "I don't know about him."

She turned back to Gran. "Look, Mr. Tucker can't have gone far. Not in the state he's in."

"What state is he in?" said Gran. "Just how sick is he?"

"He's got malaria, you know," said the nurse. "It's a very dangerous disease."

"Just give me a straight answer," said Gran.

The nurse pursed her lips. She flashed a glance at Firebird, as if wondering whether to speak the truth in front of the child.

"Sometimes people with malaria pass away," she said, "although we try our very best."

And then she went flying off down the corridor.

Firebird frowned. It hadn't sunk in yet what the nurse actually meant. Down in the swamp, where they gutted and skinned eels every day, they didn't use euphemisms for death.

"Pass away?" said Firebird. "Does that mean die?"

"Yep," said Gran. "That's what it means."

Firebird was silent.

Gran said, "What the hell's he up to, wandering off like that? And what about Ford?"

"Do you think they went home?" said Firebird in a small, quiet voice. "Back to the swamp?"

"Bet you're right," said Gran, grim faced. "I wouldn't put anything past those two. They're both as pigheaded as each other. But we've got to get your dad back here." Gran hauled herself out of her chair. "His best chance is back here."

"Dad's not going to die, is he?" Firebird burst out, finally daring to ask the question.

But she didn't get the reassurance she needed. Something was happening to Gran. Her face had turned sweaty gray. Her legs buckled. And her big body was just folding to the floor like a floppy rag doll. She tried to hold on to a chair, but it crashed down with her.

"Gran!" Firebird knelt down beside her, shook her. Gran's eyes didn't open. Firebird went rushing to the door, screaming, "Help! My gran's sick!"

People heard and they came running. Firebird stood in the corner of the waiting room, shaking, crying, while they clustered around Gran, shouting instructions to one another and loaded her onto a gurney. Firebird knew Gran wasn't dead because she was moaning.

At the last moment someone remembered that Firebird was there. A nurse turned back.

"It's all right," she said to Firebird. "We'll look after her." Then she was gone, too, and all Firebird could hear were the wheels squeaking as they took Gran away.

Firebird was left alone—a tiny figure hunched in a corner, in a cell-like room, in a huge hospital in the middle of the city, with just a TV for company.

She didn't know what to do now. They'd taken Gran away somewhere and Ford and Dad had gone back to the swamp without her. There was no one to turn to.

Then Firebird realized she was still clutching some sticky coins in her fist, along with the piece of paper. She looked down at Loreal's message: *If you need help . . .*

Firebird found a pay phone in the hospital corridor. She wasn't sure how to use it. Her hands were trembling. She dropped one of the coins. There was a man waiting behind her; that made her even more awkward. He was frowning, wanting her to hurry. She didn't know how much money to use. She fed in all her coins, feverishly punched in the number, and clamped the phone to her ear.

Somewhere, it seemed at the end of a long tunnel, a phone was ringing.

When a woman's voice said, "Hello," Firebird felt her heart would stop beating. She tried to form her lips into words.

"Hello?" said the voice again.

Firebird said, hesitantly, "Mom?" She was frantically

searching in her mind for what to say next. "Gran and Dad are sick," was already on her lips. But then the faraway voice said, "I think you've got the wrong number."

The man was still watching her, staring at her. In a state of near panic Firebird blurted out, "Are you Loreal?"

"Loreal's at work," said the voice. "Have you got her cell number? Try her at the Union Theater." And the phone went dead.

"Hello?" said Firebird. "Hello?" But all she got was a long, wailing tone.

"Are you finished now?" said the man, moving toward her.

Firebird dropped the receiver, let it dangle on the wire, and took off toward the safety of the elevators.

She tried to calm herself as the elevator slid down. She had no other phone numbers and no more money. But whoever it was on the end of the line had given her an address: the Union Theater. She felt a step closer to Mom.

Firebird went up to the reception desk. It was against everything Gran and Trapper had taught her—to trust in the kindness of strangers—but Firebird didn't have a choice.

"Please," she asked, "can you tell me how to get to the Union Theater?"

Then Firebird was back on the city streets, with the receptionist's directions in her head.

PEOPLE were still rushing home from work. There was traffic gridlock, horns blaring. But Firebird slipped through the cars and crowds like a wraith. She felt sick with anticipation.

Her mind was having to make huge readjustments. Mom wasn't an angel in heaven, but a real, living, breathing person. *What does she look like?* thought Firebird. When she tried to imagine Mom, she kept seeing the stone angel's face—a face that was beautiful, but as cold and remote as the moon.

Suddenly, Firebird stopped dead. Someone almost crashed into her. "Hey, get out of the way."

Firebird didn't even hear them. *What am I doing?* she was thinking. *I must be crazy.* Going to see a total stranger who'd walked out on them years ago. Why should she help now? Why should she care?

Firebird, torn by so many conflicting feelings, nearly turned back to the swamp.

She even stopped, gazed upward, seeking out the city's tallest tower. If she found that, she could get back to the plaza and down into the subways.

There it was, the tower, soaring into the gray evening sky, high above the other buildings.

And suddenly, it was lit up. Lights were twinkling all over it. But there was no beam from the roof, trawling the sky to catch migrating birds. There'd be no golden oriole, hummingbird, or parakeet bodies littering the plaza tonight.

That's because of me, thought Firebird. *I did that.*

That made her proud, like she'd made a difference. And somehow it gave her the courage not to scurry back to the swamp.

Go find Mom, Firebird decided. *And if she doesn't want to help, fine. Just tell her to go to hell. Tell her we don't need her anyway.*

Besides, Firebird told herself, *you're nearly there now.*

There was the big drive-through McDonald's. Turn right by that, the receptionist said, and Union Theater was just down the street.

Firebird could see it as soon as she turned the corner. It was a grand building, with columns at the front and UNION THEATER on a big banner that hung outside. When she got closer she saw posters with swirling dancers on them advertising tonight's show.

But the theater was still dark, closed up. Firebird peered through the glass doors.

Nobody in there, she thought. Her heart sank. But at the same time she felt relieved.

"Doors don't open until eight," said someone behind her. Firebird spun around. This time she didn't run or hide. It was a woman with chunky amber beads around her neck. Friendly faced, but way too old to be Mom.

"I'm looking for Loreal," said Firebird.

She steeled herself for the woman to say, "Who?" because Firebird was filled again with crippling doubts. Her mind was spinning off into wild suspicions. Gran had seemed so sincere back in the waiting room as if it was an end to all the lies. As if she were finally telling Firebird the truth. But what if she wasn't and this was just another layer of lies on top of all the others? What if Gran had set this all up somehow for her own twisted reasons, sent Firebird on a wild-goose chase? Maybe Mom wasn't in the city at all. Maybe she wasn't even still alive. . . .

"You want to see Loreal?" said the woman. "No problem. She'll be with the costumes. I'll take you in the back way."

Then everything happened way too fast, like a speeded-up film. The woman took Firebird in by a back door, through some cramped corridors, and left her outside a door labeled WARDROBE.

"Sorry," she said, "got to dash. You'll find Loreal in there."

Firebird stood alone, staring at the closed door, with a yearning inside her that was so sharp and intense it felt like pain.

Remember, Mom walked out on you, Firebird warned herself. How could she feel so needy, yet so hurt and angry at the same time?

Very gently, she pushed the door open and peered inside.

At first she was confused by all the clutter crammed into one tiny space—a washing machine, racks of clothes, paints, spray cans, brushes, and boxes full of stuff. Then her eyes sorted out a person sitting at a table spread with bright fabrics, chopping away at something with big scissors. Instantly Firebird had the strangest flashback. She saw herself, back home in the swamp, bent over the table just like that, cutting out eel skins.

The woman had frizzy red hair like she did, and the same expression of fierce concentration. She was even biting her bottom lip, like Firebird did.

Firebird watched her working for a few seconds, her quick fingers gluing fabrics together—neat, professional.

"Mom?" she said timidly.

Loreal looked up, and her face was nothing like the stone angel's. It was flushed pink, flesh and blood. And emotions were chasing across it. Surprise, recognition, then delight.

"Firebird?" she said.

"I thought you were dead," said Firebird.

"Well, I'm alive, last I checked." Loreal smiled.

She sprang up from the table scattering glue tubes and sketches of costumes. She tried to give Firebird a hug. But Firebird's body resisted, going stiff as a plank. Loreal held her at arm's length instead and looked at her.

"Sorry," said Loreal. "I smell of stain remover."

Firebird was expecting apologies, explanations—like why Mom hadn't been part of their lives for the last thirteen years. She felt she was owed them after all the lies. But Loreal didn't do any of that. She said, "So what's going on, down at the swamp?"

Firebird just stared at her.

"I was in a taxi, going over the overpass," said Loreal. "Soon as I saw the billboard was gone, I made my driver pull up. I saw everything. Then we followed the ambulance to the hospital. They told me Trapper has malaria."

"Where have you *been* all this time?" Firebird demanded furiously.

But instead of opening that can of worms, Loreal had her own question. "Did Carol-Ann send you?"

Firebird had to think for a moment who Carol-Ann was—no one ever called Gran by her real name. "No," she said. "Gran's sick, too. And I think Ford and Dad have gone back to the swamp. And Dad should be back in the hospital . . ."

Loreal was already shrugging on a denim jacket.

"You're not sick, are you?" Loreal interrupted. "You and Ford?"

"No," said Firebird.

"You've been lucky then," said Loreal. "Lucky not to get bitten by one of those malarial mosquitoes." She shook her head, her eyes faraway. "That damn swamp."

Then she focused on Firebird. Loreal didn't talk like Gran; she didn't try to confuse you with smoke and mirrors. She cut straight to the heart of the matter. "Look, I wouldn't blame you if you hated my guts, thought I didn't love you—"

"I don't hate you," protested Firebird, horrified. "Honest, I don't!"

"Anyway," said Loreal, "like I said, I wouldn't blame you. Nobody would. And I'll try to make it up to you, I promise. But we've got other things to do first. We'd better get out to the swamp, find Ford and Trapper, and get your dad back to the hospital. Wait here just two seconds. I've got to get somebody to stand in for me during the performance." Then she rushed away.

Firebird stood, staring around, not really thinking about anything, feeling unreal. But one part of her mind was listening to voices out in the corridor. She heard Loreal say, "My daughter," and Firebird thought, in a dazed kind of way, *This is all so* weird.

Then Loreal came racing back. "All fixed," she said. She was jangling some keys. "I borrowed the stage manager's car. Told him it was an emergency."

Firebird hurried beside Loreal, giving her sly, sideways glances. She was still trying to get over the shock of her physical presence. But at the same time drinking in every tiny detail: her frayed jeans, the Band-Aid on her heel where her sandals rubbed, her bright purple toenails that clashed with her hair.

Mom's alive, Firebird thought, as if at last she believed it. *She's here, next to me now, and she's* alive.

It was Mom's nose piercing—a tiny silver stud—that finally did it. It exploded forever the myth of that other angelic dead Mom—the nice, quiet, contented, swamp-loving girl. Exploded it and sent it spinning off into infinity, like space junk.

In this crazy, surreal situation, Firebird was having crazy thoughts. *You couldn't imagine that old angel getting her nose pierced, or painting her toenails purple. She wouldn't be seen dead in that color*, thought Firebird, but then remembered that angels are dead already.

"You know that stone angel in Willow Creek? They told us that was your memorial," said Firebird breathlessly as she hurried to keep up with Mom.

Loreal was looking down the street to see where the stage manager's car was parked. But she turned and stared at Firebird. "Did they?" She seemed almost amused. "That piece of old junk? You know, I hated that angel when I was little. I always thought she had a real snooty face."

21

Deep in the swamp, Ford sat hunched up in the reeds, waiting, like Trapper had told him to. The fuel cans were lined up on the bank, the boat moored in the creek. And Trapper was still propped up behind him against the tree.

It wasn't dark yet. But it never got fully dark in the swamp because of light pollution from the city. Just like it was never totally silent because of the traffic's constant roar.

The city lights were already coming on, staining the sky over the towers lurid orange, red, and green. But Ford suddenly noticed there was no searchlight from the tallest tower sweeping the sky.

Firebird was telling the truth, thought Ford, amazed. *She did go up there and smash that thing.* He realized he'd got Firebird all wrong. He thought she was a lazy dreamer who just drifted around all day in her own little world. But it turned out his twin sister was full of surprises.

But Ford didn't like looking at the city, especially since he and Dad had just escaped from it. He preferred to blank all that out of his mind. And the hospital, too, as if Trapper had never been taken there.

Instead, he lowered his gaze and stared around him. The swamp was spooky just before nightfall. Still and brooding, like it was waiting for something. Everything blurred into fuzzy gray. Fireflies flickered around, whizzing pinpoints of light. There were strange noises, rustlings, chirrupings, the soft croaking of frogs. Most creatures in the swamp went out hunting at night.

There was a rustle in the reeds. Was it Swamp Dog? Without Swamp Dog they never would have found their way back.

"Here, boy," called Ford. His own voice sounded eerie, echoing. "Come here, boy." But Swamp Dog was keeping an even lower profile than usual. There was no sign of him. No nose poking out from the reeds, or even his skinny backside as he ran away.

Ford shivered. "You cold, Dad?" It was getting chilly. At least it meant the mosquitoes had stopped biting.

To ease his fears and loneliness, he started talking over his shoulder to Trapper.

"I expect Hog'll come back," said Ford, chucking little stones one by one into the creek from a pile he'd made beside him. "He can't have gone far, Dad. He's too lazy to hunt for his own dinner." Ford thought it was time to cheer Dad up, make him look on the bright side. "They'll put the billboard back, you'll see, Dad." *Plop.* Ford chucked in another stone, watched it sink in a ring of ripples. "And when you get better, Dad, we'll go out trapping eels again, you and me. We'll catch some great big 'uns."

But there was something else on his mind. He wanted to reassure Trapper about that, too—that he didn't mind about the lies. That he knew Trapper had only been telling them to protect him. That he understood about his pride.

"Look, Dad," Ford started, "I know about the smokery closing down and you dumping out the eels. I know where the money's been coming from—from selling Firebird's purses in the city. But it doesn't matter, Dad. Honest, who cares? Business'll get good again. It's got to . . ."

Trapper was being terribly quiet, even for him. Ford stopped talking and sinking stones into the creek. He looked around.

"Dad!"

Trapper's cigarette was burned out, still dangling between limp fingers. His head was thrown back, his face pointing up to heaven, his eyes closed, his mouth open.

Ford leaped up, ran over, and shook him. Trapper's head lolled forward onto his chest. But then he raised it again, opened his eyes, and looked blurrily at Ford.

"Dad," said Ford, almost weeping with relief and gratitude. "I thought . . . I thought . . ."

But then Trapper said, "You hear that boat engine?" He staggered to his feet like a drunk man. "They're coming. Knew they would," he said to Ford, nodding like he'd been proven right.

Ford listened. But he couldn't hear any boat engine.

"Hand me that fuel can," said Trapper. He started unscrewing the top feverishly. Ford could smell the sudden stink of gasoline.

"What you going to do, Dad?" whispered Ford, suddenly uneasy.

Trapper snaked through the reeds. Then he started pouring gasoline into Willow Creek, a whole canful of it. The sluggish current carried the fuel slick into the heart of the swamp, away from their boat. The gasoline looked almost pretty, iridescent with rainbows, shimmering with blues, purples, and greens. Ford watched it, as if in a dream, spreading out on the water surface, drifting downstream toward Loreal's angel.

Trapper's can was empty. He flung it away, stumbled back to Ford, grasped his arm, and thrust his sweating face close to Ford's.

"If they think they're going to get my swamp," hissed Trapper, "they're making a big mistake."

He took his lighter out of his pocket.

"No, Dad," said Ford. "You'll burn the whole swamp."

"That's what I aim to do," said Trapper. "If we can't have it, no one can."

Ford looked at him, shocked, unbelieving. "I thought you said we'd fight 'em?"

Trapper gripped Ford's arm even tighter, fixing him with fierce, delirious eyes. "Listen to me, son! Are you listening?"

"Yes, Dad," said Ford, even though he felt half crazy, too, with fear and horror.

"We're finished here, son," raved Trapper. "There's no future for us here, no home anymore. I'm telling you the truth now. Listen, there are more of the bastards coming."

In the background, Ford could hear sirens wailing.

"There's always sirens in the city," Ford pleaded. "Dad, that doesn't mean they're coming here."

But Trapper was beyond all reason, in some kind of nightmare place where Ford couldn't reach him. Dad flicked on his lighter, then seemed to change his mind. He flicked it off again and picked up another can. He was chuckling gleefully to himself. "Got to make a good fire, so everyone in that damn city will see it."

"What about that boat engine you just heard?" Ford said, frantically. "What if there is someone coming?"

"Burn 'em!" said Trapper, froth on his lips. "Burn the bastards!"

But he never even managed to twist off the top of the can, because suddenly he lost his balance and went tumbling down the bank into their boat. He sprawled on the bottom, perfectly still.

Ford went scrambling down the bank after him and crouched beside him in the boat. "Dad?" But even now Trapper wasn't beaten. He opened hot, feverish eyes, lifted a trembling hand. He still had the lighter clenched in his fist.

"Here," he said to Ford. "Finish the job for me. Burn the whole damn place."

Ford couldn't speak. "Do it!" begged Trapper, clutching Ford's sleeve with a feeble hand, his strength gone. But he still managed to raise his head and stare into Ford's face. "Do it, son. I'm depending on you. You're my right-hand man."

Ford was weeping now, but he sobbed, "Okay, Dad, okay," and he took the lighter.

Trapper laid his head back peacefully on the deck boards, as if a great burden had been lifted from him. As if, at last, he was free of the swamp and the daily nightmare of worrying about it and the violent thoughts and acts it had driven him to.

"Okay, Dad," said Ford again, even though Trapper's eyes were closed and he didn't seem to be listening. "I'll do it. Look, I'm going to do it now."

"Wait," came Trapper's feeble voice from the bottom of the boat. He opened his eyes.

"What, Dad?" Ford had to lean down very close to hear what Trapper was telling him. His voice came again, just a whisper from pale lips.

Now that Trapper had started truth telling, it seemed he felt an urgent need to explain everything to Ford. Even if it was the last thing he ever did.

"You've got to let this place go," he said to Ford. "Let it go. Move on . . ."

Ford smeared his face with the back of his hand so Dad wouldn't see the tears, then crouched back again to listen.

Trapper's strength was gone. But along with his failing breath, a few more words came from his lips. "Gran'll take care of you. And your mother. It wasn't her fault, you remember that . . ."

"What, Dad?" Ford squeezed Trapper's hand. "What?"

Now his hot tears were falling on Trapper's face. But not a nerve twitched, not a muscle moved. Dad looked so calm, so rested, as if he had no worries in the world.

But Ford was yelling, shaking Dad, trying to lift him up and make him come alive again. The boat rocked wildly.

Ford felt for a pulse—none. No breath, no heartbeat. And looking at his empty face Ford could see it wasn't him at all. That Dad seemed already to have left his body. And Ford had to finally accept that Trapper had died.

Ford laid him down, very gently, on the deck boards. He watched him for a long time and pushed Trapper's hair back off his cold forehead so he could study his face.

Then gradually Ford became aware that he was still gripping Dad's lighter.

Suddenly, a mad frenzy seemed to overtake him. What had he been thinking of, just sitting there? Dad had asked him to do something.

He scrambled out of the boat, ran down the bank, and flicked on the lighter. He was looking around wildly for what to torch first when the lighter slipped from his greasy fingers and did the job for him. Flames spurted. Instantly, they had a life of their own. A greedy little fire raced down the bank toward the fuel slick in the creek.

With a blinding flare, the creek ignited. Ford stared at it, like a rabbit caught in car headlights, his tearstained face red in the reflected glow. The fire was breaking up into fiery islands on the water. A sudden rush of wind sent one spinning away. It was fanned along the creek, a little floating fire. Ford watched it, mesmerized. He tried to run, but suddenly his limbs wouldn't obey him. He couldn't stop his legs from shaking. He thought he was going to collapse.

The fire was heading straight for the boat.

The first thing it did was burn off the mooring rope. The boat began to drift along the creek with the fire circling it, like red water lilies. It picked up speed. Somewhere in the distant ocean, the tide was going out, pulling the boat toward it. Then the boat began to burn, the fire flickering up the sides, taking hold.

It was glowing crimson now in the darkness, riding down to the river like a Viking funeral pyre. Seconds passed when Ford couldn't see it. The boat must be out of the swamp by now, in the river's wide, open spaces.

Then the fire found the fuel tank. Ford heard the distant boom, saw the brilliant white flash as the boat was incinerated, with Dad's body onboard. He sank down onto the bank, overwhelmed with grief and horror. At that moment, he didn't care if he lived or died.

But then the fire crackled nearer. He felt its heat. Smoke crept into his lungs; he was coughing. The fire was scorching him, blistering his skin. The pain made him howl like a wounded beast and shocked him into action. The instinct for survival kicked in.

His mind was just red, molten panic. He fled from the fire with speed and strength he didn't know he possessed. He leaped creeks, dodging walls of flames as they writhed this way and that. He broke through the choking black smoke into clear air.

At last, down by the river, he crouched on a muddy bank, shivering with cold and shock. He was safe, but he couldn't have cared less about that. He looked back. Over the swamp it seemed as if the sky, too, was on fire. As if the whole world was burning up.

22

LOREAL swerved off onto the hard shoulder of the highway and switched off the car engine. It was dark now, or as dark as it ever got near the city. Freight trucks screamed by in a blaze of lights, making the car shake.

Loreal peered out of the windshield. "Think we're anywhere near the swamp yet?" she asked Firebird. It was hard to get their bearings with no billboard dominating the night sky like a giant cinema screen.

All they could see beyond the highway were spiky bushes. Firebird thought the branches had white blossoms—until she realized they were hundreds of torn plastic bags caught on the thorns. But only a few feet from the car, the bushes dissolved into murky shadows.

Loreal said, "We'd better leave the car here." The ambulance had driven right up to the swamp. But she knew the car couldn't handle that rough terrain.

On the drive from the city Firebird had said nothing. As if she was afraid to let her feelings out. As if she was holding them very carefully, like you would a glass filled to the brim, scared that it'd spill.

Loreal had talked just to break the awkward silence, given Firebird a quick rundown of her life since the swamp. How she'd worked her way up from a humble stitcher in the wardrobe department of a dance company. How she was in charge of looking after their costumes now. How they'd even let her design and make some of them. How it was her dream, someday soon, to start her own costume-design business.

Firebird had stayed silent. But in her mind, as Mom was talking, was the billboard's message: "LIVE YOUR DREAMS!"

Loreal had told Firebird how she'd been away for years touring with the dance company all over the world—Russia, Italy, Australia, China.

And Firebird saw in her mind all those faraway places on the billboard, places she'd thought a girl from the swamp would never get to see.

"But there wasn't a day that passed," Loreal had said, "when I didn't think of you and Ford."

At last Firebird's feelings had spilled over. "So why didn't you ever try to get in touch?" she'd demanded.

It wasn't a good time to have a heart-to-heart. Loreal was switching lanes, concentrating on the traffic.

"I wasn't here," she'd said, staring ahead through the windshield, her hands gripping the wheel very tight. "I wasn't even in this country most of the time."

"You could've sent me a postcard!" Firebird had protested, thinking immediately, *That's a dumb thing to say,* because their house never got mail; it didn't even have a postal address.

"Well, not a postcard," she'd corrected herself. "But you could've got in touch *somehow*."

"Yes, I could have," Loreal had admitted. "But the truth is, I didn't think I had the right. Because I'd left you behind, I didn't think you'd want to know me. Best for you to believe that I was dead."

"No, it wasn't," Firebird had burst out. "It wasn't best. That's what *Gran* said. But it *wasn't*."

And then there'd been silence again in the car, until Loreal had swerved on to the hard shoulder, trying to find the swamp.

Now Loreal was saying, "You coming?" She had her hand on the door handle, ready to get out of the car.

But there was one question that Firebird had to let out, or she felt it might explode inside her brain. "Where does my name come from?"

"What?" said Loreal, letting go of the door handle and turning to stare at her daughter.

The car rocked as another freight truck thundered by.

"Didn't they tell you?" said Loreal.

"Gran said she named me after a car ad on the billboard, a Pontiac Firebird. A big, red one, with tail fins."

Loreal shook her head. "That Carol-Ann, she thinks up some wonderful stories . . ."

"They're *lies*," insisted Firebird. "Because I wasn't named after an ad on the billboard, was I?"

"Oh yes, you were," said Loreal. "Only it wasn't a car ad. And she didn't name you, I did."

"*You* did?" Firebird swiveled around. In the dark little cocoon of the car, she couldn't see the expression in Loreal's eyes.

"Did your gran tell you about a red dress I used to wear around the swamp? That I made for myself?"

"Yes," said Firebird, "she told me about that."

"See?" said Loreal. "She didn't tell you lies all the time."

Firebird frowned, as if that wasn't what she wanted to hear.

"Anyway," said Loreal, "I first saw that dress in an ad on the billboard—I must've been about twelve years old. The ad was for a dance company coming to the city. And they were doing a ballet, Stravinsky's *Firebird*. And the woman dancing the part of the firebird, she was on the billboard. She wore this amazing red dress, all red feathers like flames. It just knocked me out, that poster—I cried when they came to take it down. It was maybe four years after that when you and Ford were born. But I remembered that ad and you had silky red hair, just the same color as that dancer's dress. And that's what I named you, Firebird. And Trapper, he named Ford after a truck—but I didn't have any say in that."

"What happened to the red dress you made?" asked Firebird.

"Oh, I don't know," said Loreal, surprised by the question. "I suppose I wore it until it fell to pieces."

Firebird was silent, as if she was turning over all this new information in her mind to see how she liked it.

"And when I went to the city," added Loreal, "the billboard helped me again. I didn't know a living soul. But I'd spent so long staring at that *Firebird* ad, I knew the name of that dance company by heart, even their phone number. I called them and asked them for a job—can you believe it? For heaven's sake, I didn't even know how to use a pay phone . . ."

Suddenly, Loreal stopped short, gave herself a shake, as if she'd got carried away. "Look," she said, "you don't want to hear all this now. We have to find your dad and Ford."

But Firebird was thinking new, surprising thoughts. *It wasn't all lies*, she was telling herself. Her name did come from the billboard after all. Not from a flashy red car, but a dancer in a Firebird costume. And it wasn't a lie when the billboard said "LIVE YOUR DREAMS!" Because Loreal had gone and done it.

"We'd better go," said Loreal.

Together, they got out of the car and struggled up through the scratchy scrubland.

Loreal was wondering if they'd stopped in the right place—it had been hard to tell in the dark. Then suddenly, ahead of them, they saw smoke rising and a sinister, crimson glow.

The glow lit up the gap where the billboard had been.

"The swamp's that way," said Firebird. They were both running now, crashing through scrubland. Firebird felt a sickening sense of foreboding.

The gap left by the billboard was like the gateway to hell. Beyond it was a fiery sea. That was the swamp grass burning. Willow trees blazed like smoking torches. Piles of storm debris were white-hot bonfires.

"My god," said Loreal as she and Firebird stared in horror. "The whole swamp is burning, right down to the river."

She hardly recognized the place where she'd been brought up in. A bloodred sky reflected the fiery swamp. A column of black smoke spiraled up and spread out in a mushroom cloud.

Bet you can see that for miles, thought Loreal.

Firebird was already picking her way across the billboard, almost invisible now under a layer of silt and ash.

"No, don't go any farther," warned Loreal. "It's not safe."

"But what about Dad and Ford?"

Loreal was already pressing numbers on her cell phone. "I'm calling the fire department," she said. The flames hadn't reached the Tuckers' house yet. *If they come quick,* thought Loreal, *they might save it.*

Then they heard sirens coming closer, getting louder. The first fire engine came tearing up through the scrubland, blue lights flashing.

"No need to call," said Loreal, putting away her cell phone. "They're already here."

23

IN MINUTES, the emergency services had taken charge of the situation. The city was in danger. The fire had to be controlled at all costs.

The swamp was crawling with firefighters, police, and officials from other government departments all rushing around excitedly, shouting orders to one another, talking into radios. The Tuckers' yard was crammed with their vehicles. Suddenly the swamp was everyone's business.

Helicopters water bombed the fire, dousing the fiercest flames. Now teams of men with long-handled rubber paddles were moving through the swamp, beating out every last spark. They'd saved the house, then taken it over as their headquarters, stomping on Gran's scrubbed floors with their big, muddy boots.

Helicopters still buzzed overhead. But these were hired by TV stations. The fire made spectacular viewing. It was a big news item. Trapper had always guarded the family's privacy so fiercely, but now pictures of the Tuckers' little empire were being relayed live on national TV.

In the shadowy house, lit only by oil lamps, Loreal and Firebird hovered in the background, trying not to get in the way.

The swamp was giving up all of its secrets. A firefighter came crashing through the door, helped himself to coffee in one of Gran's best china cups, and flopped down on one of her chintzy chairs.

His face was streaked with black sweat. He smeared it off with the flat of his hand. Then he said, "There's some kind of statue out there in one of the creeks. Really spooked me, staring up at me like that. Thought it was somebody drowned."

Loreal stepped up to him. "Excuse me," she said, "my son and his dad are still missing."

In all the panic about a threat to the city, Ford and Trapper seemed to have been forgotten.

"Well, there's no sign of them out there," said the firefighter. "Did they have a boat?"

Firebird nodded dumbly.

"This your daughter?" the firefighter asked Loreal.

And when Loreal said, very firmly, "Yes, this is my daughter," he seemed surprised that Firebird looked so stunned, as if it was a big discovery.

"Anyhow, you shouldn't be worried," the firefighter said. "If they had any sense, soon as this fire started, they'd have made a run for the river. They'll be heading back soon. Fire's almost out now—just a few little pockets still smoldering."

A guy with FWS on his padded jacket was listening in. It was Beardface—and he hadn't forgotten Trapper.

"You talking about that eel fisher?" he said. "There's some questions I'd like to ask him about a smashed solar panel."

He wanted more information, but Loreal and Firebird shrank back into Gran's bedroom and closed the door on the chaos outside.

Where are they? thought Firebird, her face pale with worry.

She sneaked a look at Loreal. She was worried, too, on edge, pacing about the bedroom. Every time Firebird looked at her, she was amazed all over again. She had to keep reminding herself, *That's my mom.* And each time she did, it seemed like a miracle.

From Gran's bedroom window, Firebird could see a long line of bobbing lights. It was the safety lamps on the firefighters' helmets. They were in the very heart of the swamp, in its most hidden, mysterious places. They must have found Hog's pool by now.

With everything else happening, the great white eel had slipped Firebird's mind. He was a mean, snappy old devil sometimes. He rang that bell like the Tuckers were his servants and he was some kind of royalty. But she thought, *I hope the fire didn't kill him.* She pictured him, hiding out from the fire in the cool depths of his pool, his white coils glimmering in the dark.

She watched Loreal pacing around.

"Do you think you and Dad could ever get back together?" asked Firebird. She kept her voice casual, but her heart was thumping. Loreal saw the hope in Firebird's eyes. She came and stood right in front of her daughter, and looked her straight in the face.

"I'm sorry, Firebird," said Loreal. "But I've got to tell you the truth. I just can't see that happening. I mean, not ever. Even if *I* wanted to, he wouldn't want *me*."

She could see Firebird wasn't convinced. She changed the subject. "What about Ford?" she said. "Does he know about me? That I'm still alive?"

Firebird shook her head.

"What do you think he'll say, when he knows?" asked Loreal. She looked really worried about that. "Your dad never forgave me for leaving," she added.

Firebird had been wondering about that, too—how Ford would react. Ford was fiercely loyal to Dad. What was he going to think of Loreal, once he'd got over the shock of having a real live mom? Firebird thought, *I know whose side he'll be on.*

The door to the bedroom burst open. "Excuse me," said a man in uniform. "But we're done here. We're just packing up to leave. Fire's finally out. There's no danger to the city now."

Firebird stood at the window, watching the emergency vehicles, in convoy, head back down over the scrubland. Only when the last one had left the yard did she go out into the kitchen. She closed the back door that they'd left flapping open.

Loreal was calling the hospital again to check on Gran. She'd tried several times before, but the line was busy. This time she was lucky.

Firebird could hear a voice gabbling at the other end. But she had no idea what it was saying. Then she saw relief spreading over Mom's face.

Loreal told Firebird, "Your gran hasn't got malaria. She just fainted, that's all."

"Fainted?" repeated Firebird. "You sure?" Words like *fainted* and tough women like Gran didn't seem to go together.

Loreal nodded. "Everything got to be too much for her, I suppose. Anyway, she hasn't got malaria, they're sure about that. She's sitting up, drinking a cup of tea, and ordering everyone around—that's my Carol-Ann."

"Tell her," said Loreal, speaking into the phone again. "Tell her that her granddaughter's fine. Tell her that she's with her mom and not to worry about her. Be sure to tell her that, won't you?"

Firebird examined her feelings. And she found that she was really glad Gran was okay after all. Gran had lied a lot, told her all sorts of crap. Firebird was still outraged about that—wasn't ready to forgive. But, in her heart, she knew Gran had been between a rock and a hard place, torn between Loreal and Trapper. Firebird was beginning to appreciate just how that felt.

Loreal said to Firebird, "All we've got to worry about now is your dad—and Ford."

And suddenly, Firebird felt a sliver of ice in her heart. She stared coldly at Loreal. She felt resentment again, surging through her, as if she was on a roller coaster of emotion.

"You didn't worry about them for thirteen years," she challenged Loreal. "So why are you worried now?"

"I *did* worry." Loreal shook her head helplessly. "I worried about you all every day, especially you and Ford." She stopped herself saying just in time, "I did what I thought was best for you both." Firebird had already poured scorn on *that* idea.

But Firebird turned away and walked over to the window. With her back ramrod straight, unyielding, she stared across the fire-blasted swamp to the river beyond.

And thought she saw a slouching figure.

She screwed up her eyes, looked again. "There's someone out there," she told Loreal.

"Who is it?" said Loreal anxiously, running to join her at the window.

"It's Ford," said Firebird. She was certain of it. "I'm going to get him." She was already running toward the back door.

"Is Trapper with him?" asked Loreal. "Wait, I'll come with you."

Firebird turned. "No," she said. "No. You stay here."

And then she was running away from Loreal, across the kitchen and out of the back door.

24

THERE was nowhere to hide in the swamp anymore, no hidden dens or secret places. It had all been burned down to stubble in the fierce inferno. The ground still felt hot as Firebird set out to meet Ford. Crispy sundews crunched under her feet. The islands were heaps of gray ash, the willows charcoal. And over everything hung the sickening stench of the fire.

Moonlight, city lights, and the lack of cover made it easy to see Ford. There he was in the distance, a small, hunched figure. He was sitting on the bank of a creek. Was it Willow Creek? Firebird couldn't tell anymore; now the familiar landmarks she'd known all her life had gone and the whole swamp looked the same—a smoking, blackened wasteland.

"Where's Dad?" was the first thing Firebird asked Ford.

Ford hung his head, wouldn't even look at her. He wasn't crying anymore. For the moment he'd cried himself out.

"Where's Dad?" asked Firebird again, already feeling sick with dread.

This time Ford turned his tragic face toward her. Still Firebird wouldn't believe what that face was telling her.

"Dad has to get back to the hospital," she said.

"Dad died," said Ford. And even though he felt out of his mind with grief, somewhere inside him a small, triumphant voice was saying, *At least he didn't die in that hospital, stuck full of needles, dressed in too-big baby clothes! At least he died in the boat that was his pride and joy. And I was with him*, thought Ford. *Nobody else.* He felt that was a kind of privilege.

Firebird stared at Ford, horror spreading over her face. "What happened? Did he die in the fire?"

"No," said Ford. "He was so sick. He just died in the boat. And then the swamp started burning. And the boat burned, too, with Dad in it."

He didn't tell Firebird how the fire had started. That had been Dad's last request to him personally and nobody else's business, not even Firebird's.

There was a long, long silence while Firebird struggled to take in what Ford had told her, and Ford kept seeing Dad's face in his mind, peaceful, in the bottom of the boat, all the anger and bitterness smoothed out of it.

"I can't believe it," said Firebird. "I can't believe he's dead."

"I know," said Ford.

But he didn't think her loss was as great as his. He'd been closest to Dad, closer than anyone. He couldn't believe he'd ever be happy again or that the pain inside him would ever stop.

"We've got to tell Gran," said Firebird.

Ford got wearily to his feet. "Come on, boy," he said.

A skinny, lizard-headed hound came slinking out of the reeds.

Firebird said, amazed, "It's Swamp Dog!"

Ford said, "He should've been a cat—he's got nine lives." Swamp Dog always came back, he was a real survivor. Ford reached down to scratch Swamp Dog behind the ears.

Then he was telling Firebird about Dad's last words. Ford had been puzzling over them. He felt bound to follow Dad's wishes—if he could only figure out what Dad meant.

"Before Dad died, he said something weird. He said about Gran looking after us. But he said Mom would, too. And he said that it wasn't her fault. And that I had to remember that. Does that make any sense to you?" Ford shook his head, sighing. "Dad probably didn't know what he was saying."

Oh yes, he did, thought Firebird. Then she thought, *You've got to tell Ford about Mom.*

In a minute she would, before they reached the house, so he'd know who Loreal was when she came running out to meet them.

She trudged silently over the scorched earth with Ford beside her, Swamp Dog at his heels.

"Dad said we're finished here," said Ford. "He said that even before the fire, when Hog left."

"Hog left?" said Firebird.

That hardly seemed important at all. Not when she still couldn't accept that she'd never see Trapper again.

"Dad was right," Firebird told Ford. "We can't stay here."

It wasn't the fire that would force them out. She'd heard those FWS officials talking back at the house—they'd said the swamp would recover from that. It had even done them a favor, frying some of those malarial mosquitoes. It wasn't even the fact that the billboard had fallen. That hardly seemed to matter, either, not now that the swamp had been on TV. It was something else the FWS guys had said that sealed the Tuckers' fate. Dr. Pinker had said the same thing, too. "This swamp won't be here long," they'd said. "Next week, or next year, the rising sea levels will drown it."

"What's going to happen to us?" Ford was saying. "Without Dad?" Ford felt that he'd lost half of himself. He couldn't imagine how he could carry on.

"I don't know," said Firebird truthfully.

But crazily, sneaking into her mind, came an image of Loreal so vividly alive. Her purple toenails, the Band-Aid on her heel, her nose stud, her straight talking. Firebird felt really guilty about it. Dad was dead and she was thinking about Mom. A mom she'd only just met. But she couldn't help it.

"And where are we going to go?" asked Ford. "Dad said, move on. But where to?"

Right now, Ford couldn't see any future, not without Trapper. Even when Ford was a grown man and boss of his own fishing business, he'd still think of Trapper, almost every day, and tell his own kids stories about their granddad, the legend.

"I don't know," said Firebird. "I don't know what's going to happen."

Then, from above them, Firebird heard bird calls. Black against the moon was a flock of migrating parakeets. They streamed overhead, heading for the city. But there was no beam to pull them in, send them plunging down between the city towers. Tonight, at least, they'd fly safely over.

And somewhere, in all her sadness, Firebird felt hope. She knew Ford thought his life had closed down. But she felt that hers was opening up. She wanted to tell Ford, "It'll be all right," but she knew that, right now, he wouldn't believe her.

She thought of Loreal, waiting for them back at the house. She thought of her purses displayed in the plaza like they were works of art.

And even though it was flattened into the mud, she heard the billboard's message. It was whispering to her, *Live your dreams, Firebird! Live your dreams!*